FREEDOM in the DISMAL

Also by Monifa Love

Poetry

Provisions

FREEDOM in the DISMAL

a novel
by

Monifa A. Love

Plover Press • Kaneohe, Hawaii • 1998

For information, address the publisher,
Plover Press, PO Box 1637, Kaneohe, Hawaii 96744

Printed and bound in the United States of America

Cover illustration: "Running to Freedom"

Library of Congress Cataloging-in-Publication Data

Love, Monifa A.
Freedom in the dismal : a novel / by Monifa A. Love.
p. cm.
ISBN 0-917635-26-4 (cloth: alk. paper). — ISBN 0-917635-27-2 (pbk. : alk. paper)
1. Afro-Americans—Fiction. I. Title.
PS3562.08476F74 1998
813′.54—dc21 97-47583
CIP

Distributed by

Academy Chicago Publishers
363 West Erie Street
Chicago, IL 60610

A portion of this book appeared originally in *International Quarterly* magazine.

Grateful acknowledgment is made to the following for permission to reprint copyrighted material. "Today is Not the Day", from THE MARVELOUS ARITHMETICS OF DISTANCE: Poems 1987–1992 by Audre Lorde. Copyright © 1993 by Audre Lorde. Reprinted by permission of W.W. Norton & Company, Inc. "8 de Septiembre", "Tus Manos", and "La Carta en El Camino" by Pablo Neruda, from THE CAPTAIN'S VERSES. Copyright ©1972 by Pablo Neruda and Donald D. Walsh. Reprinted by permission of New Directions Publishing Corp.

Without the generous support and consideration of the Florida Education Fund and the Zora Neale Hurston/Richard Wright Foundation, this work would still be in process. I would also like to thank Dr. William R. Jones and Dr. Sheila Ortiz-Taylor for their sustaining assistance.

For all of my loved ones
but most especially
for
Evans D. Hopkins
and
Ronald Tymus

This could be the day
I could slip anchor and wander
to the end of the jetty
uncoil into the waters
a vessel of light   moonglade
ride the freshets to sundown
and when I am gone
another stranger will find you
coiled on the warm sand
beached treasure   and love you
for the different stories
your seas tell
and the half-finished blossoms
growing out of my season
trail behind
with a comforting hum.

But today
is not the day.
Today.

—Audre Lorde

Voices
a
Prologue

Your own Truth Commission. Lights. Cameras. Notoriety. Days upon days of probing our insides. We show our insides gladly. All we ask is that you not eat them.

Me here. All chilren here. Maa. One hunred fordy seben year. Ash here. Cut roun me wris en ankle. Twenny one roun me head. Corn meal here. One hunred fordy seben har stone here. Ash me in me han. Warm bref en away. Me here. All chilren here. Maa. Okànràn òdí ní èmi kò gbodò ní àyà jíjá. No Maa. Heart no afraid.

It's you. You're the one. Finally hearing and seeing what's been buzzing round you all this time. We had nothing to do with it. Happening now, I mean. We've watched you pacing, wringing your hands, acting as if you were holding on to some deep, dark secret. You must know we already know. I mean if anybody really knows, we'd be the ones. Don't you think? Like Gran used to say, "Lord a mercy. The Emperor ain't never had no clothes, much less some new ones." Hm.

Speak up. Ain't no reason to act like it all ain't gonna come out in de end. Who knows more about truth and consequences than we?

Would that language were enough
to speak my sad ambivalence.

It not enough to know de word. Word gotta be acti-vated. Pepper sauce needed 'for de word 'come life. You can have strong potash. You can have all de medicine for make a body light. Mortar. White cloth. Make-do mortar. Make-do white cloth. I don ker. All got to be acti-vated to do good. Or harm.

. . . Whose turn is it?

Somebody's little baby child.

Or better yet, think of yourself as Thomas Gray with Prophet Nat in Jerusalem. Yes, you. Friend of the jailer and the jailed gratifying public curiosity. Removing doubts and conjectures from the public mind. The trusty, transcriber of full, free, and voluntary confessions. Yes,

think of yourself as Gray observing our calm, fiend-like faces, our hands stained with the blood of innocence. Yes, think that you are reporting what we pour into your ears and press into your eyes. And like Master Gray, take down our testimony mindful of the possible shock to the feelings of humanity. This way you won't dream that these words are just for you. How could they be?

Make of me, make of my words—what's the difference?
Here, everything hinges on signs.
Isn't that true for you?

If you don't quiet yourself, the words will just keep rushing at you, trying to mow you down. You won't hear nobody in particular. It can be surprising how many of them are out there, waiting their turn. And not waiting their turn, any longer. Me? I'm just here to listen. A witness for the witnesses, you might say.

She got on pas dem blackberries. Dat was sumpin. De smell of all dat dark ripeness. You know she thought she home wid her ma. Mind you, bushes taller' n you can reach en so crowded thick make you believe you still where you been runnin from. She go on down Drummon way, down where de juniper en tupe-

lo speak en de bat spring up at ya an de water all bloody. She mix some Alaga syrup in dat water. She wade de canal wid dem moccasin grabbin at her. Her ankles all swole up but she kep on, all de way to Pasquotan. Slipped right by New Lebanon en all dose mens en bobcats en everthin. Down en down en down to the sea. En den she sail back on home to our peoples. She tell me all dis in a dream. She look all silvery in dat dream. Wavin at me' n all. Kep on seein de number 12 big as day. Me, I mean, in ma dream. Now her husband, he still in dere somewheres. He never did unerstan how to change into hisself. Gotta be a fox sparrow get outta dere. Get outta here, too.

. . . It's alright if you want it. Why wouldn't you want it? Everybody needs consolation. Everybody needs to know somebody hears them. And everybody seems to need someone to be worse off. We like the getaway and the suffering. Just like you do. We like it most when we're the ones getting away. I guess that's just human.

Please. All witnesses will be heard. We know many of you have been waiting a very long time. Please hold on to your numbers. Everyone will be heard.

21. Daniel, a slave

22. Moses, a slave

23. Tom, a slave

24. Jack, a slave

25. ***Venus, a slave***

26. ***Wallace, a slave***

27. ***Thomas Hatchcock, a free negro***

28. ***Andrew, a slave***

29. ***Hubbard, a slave***

30. ***Juanita, a slave***

31. ***Mary, a slave***

32. ***Frank, a slave***

33. ***Hark, a slave***

34. ***Delsey, a slave***

35. ***Curtis, a slave***

36. ***Scipio, a slave***

37. ***Stephen, a slave***

38. ***Jacob, a slave***

39. ***Isaac, a slave***

40. ***Sam, a slave***

41. ***Lark, a slave***

42. ***Nelson, a slave***

43. ***Davy, a slave***

44. ***Bing, a slave***

45. ***Nat, a slave***

46. ***Dred, a slave***

47. ***Arnold Artes, a free man of color***

48. ***Nathan, a slave***

50. ***Nathaniel, a slave***

51. *Hardy, a slave*

52. *Isham, a slave*

53. *Hugh, a slave*

54. *Jim, a slave*

55. *Henry, a slave*

56. *Mosley, a free man of color*

57. *Lucy, a slave*

58. *Elizabeth Crathenton, a free woman*

59. *Christian, a slave*

60. *Exum Artist, a free man of color*

61. *Bird, a slave*

That's where they live now. In that little house overlookin the water. They still live apart but their together dream selves live right there, by the sea. It's their compromise for their frailties. After all, to do more, one of them'd probably get hurt.

People are supposed to take turns. And in their minds, they are taking turns. It's just not a tidy process. There's a long line. Usually, there are quite a few interruptions. Some folks just can't wait. Not a second longer. So we at least have to call their names. Things are pretty backed up.

It's not as if we can go in chronological order. We can't really go in any order. We tried prioritizing people's sorrows and we tried going alphabetically but we had so many arguments about whose pain weighed the most and whose name was what, we settled on a more improvisational approach.

The people who are testifying have a tendency to tell you more than you want to know about some things and less than you need to know about others. They think they'll only have this one opportunity to be understood. They may be right.

I'm exaggerating but sometimes it feels as if every little piece of them is flying at you. They are anxious to tell their stories but when it comes time for their testimony, they're still piecing it together, trying to understand what happened and why. They forget they are talking to us. We forget sometimes, too.

Stories get tangled. It's not their memory that's the problem. It's time. They back into it. It's a snare and we all get caught. They forget they are talking to us. We forget sometimes, too.

We say we have guidelines but the truth is we haven't been able to come up with any real procedures. You have to go by instinct and what seems fair. They really don't want you to be impartial. They want you to witness with your soul. Yes indeed, they do.

. . . More than they're hurt already, you know?

How in the hell am I supposed to tell you somethin in this language? Tell you somethin important like who I am? Oh yeah, you can buy and sell in it. I'm a witness to that. But tell you somethin, somethin for real . . . don't make me laugh.

You don't have to worry about me. I will use whatever language you allow. Just let me speak. Just let me be heard. It's a simple story I have to tell.

All us got a simple story.

Speak for yourself now partner.

You gonna ask what? You convene this mess and don't even know what to ask. The question is, my friends, how long?

. . . "Heard the whistle blow, couldn't see no train. Deep down in my heart, I loved you again. How long, how long, Baby, how long?"

Who's next?

FREEDOM in the DISMAL

Thursday, March 17, 1983
11:02 a.m.
Holding Cell
The Commonwealth of Virginia

Dearest R.C.—

i hope that your Mom is on the mend. i hope that you are also feeling better. i understand that you could not be with me and your mother at the same time. Please forgive my ill-considered words on the phone last night. i no longer have the luxury of my mother's presence. i forget myself. i forget that you have responsibilities other than the ones you have to me.

Delahaney has just handed down his sentence. i wish you could have been here to see the scene. All these fools dressed up in green. Green shoes, green suits, green shirts, green dresses, green carnations. Even his motherfucking honor. A "Kiss me, I'm Irish" button, no less. He made good on the promise he made 12 years ago that i'd be sorry if he ever saw me in his courtroom again. Indeed, i will not be seeing the outside until the year 2013. My droll attorney, Mr. Nichols, also dressed in green, reminded me that my stay might have been longer still. i must admit that i had not sufficiently steeled myself for Delahaney's unique anti-recidivism methodology.

There is much that you will need to do in the following weeks. Your primary focus is to monitor my transfer to the penitentiary. It is imperative that i can depend on you to call and make sure that i am all right. Knowing Delahaney, i would not be the least bit surprised if there were orders for my mistreatment. Then again, he may not give a fuck once i leave his courtroom.

i am being remanded to the facility in Richmond. You should call as soon as you receive this letter to determine my status, visitor and mail privileges, and commissary regulations. Next, you should get office supplies sent to me as soon as you have spoken to the warden. Be sure to contact *the warden. Asking questions or making requests of underlings is a trap. You will not get what we need.* Royce, *do not be afraid to solicit what we need.*

Finally, i entreat you to contact my family and make some kind of amends. i am not suggesting that the problems are your fault. Now that i have been sentenced, i don't want to have to worry about you being played against them. *Know there is no one who means more to me than you.* i have written Daddy, Cedrick, and Cat to let them know although you and i are not yet married, you are in every way my wife, and that i expect them to respect you and to discuss any and every matter relating to me with you. Attorney Nichols is still about. i will get him to mail this today so you might address these matters as soon as possible.

i love you, woman.

As always,
David

P.S. Please extend my regards to your mother and father and George. I want you to tell them everything, if you have not.

To my wife, Camille Royce Dumas

Make a home for us when it seems we have no home.
Build a bridge when it seems there is only distance.

Always,
Your husband
David Lesesne Carmichael
3/17/83

David Lesesne Carmichael,
find words for this
metaphoricalize your life
(do you like that one, metaphoricalize?)
make the unnamed things you are feeling
like something else
box them up with newspaper
let the lines from those pages
protect you
from shattering
and transform your bewildering flurry of emotions
into something you can read
look up words for this mess
this wreckage
this shambles
this confusion
this monstrosity
this ruin
you have made
of your life
you have
you
find the words
David Lee
for 30 years

maximum security
make that into something else
so it won't be what it is
your life
removed from all you want
what is it you want?
estranged as you are
from the lucky woman you have marked
with your love
life doing life doing life doing life
find the words for how you feel
like a time bomb
like china syndrome
like shit
like dead Mama Carmichael's dead baby boy
find them so you won't feel
the fear
the anxiety
the alarm
the panic
the dread
the terror
of what comes next
and what is now

62. *Luke, a slave*

63. *Charlotte, a slave*

64. *Cherry, a slave*

65. *Ben, a slave*

66. *Archer, a slave*

67. *Shadrach, a slave*

68. *Quaccoo, a slave*

69. *Preston, a slave*

70. *Becky, a slave*

71. *Ishram Turner, a free man of color*

72. *Peck, a slave*

73. *Dorcas, a slave*

74. *Delsey, a slave*

75. *Euphemia, a free woman of color*

76. *Ibby, a slave*

77. *Desdamona, a slave*

78. *Hepsey, a slave*

79. *Polite, a slave*

80. *Nonen, a slave*

81. *Scott, a slave*

82. *Minter, a slave*

83. *Armstid, a slave*

84. *Shim Camp, a free man of color*

85. *Free Bob, a free man of color*

86. *Nice Johnson, a free man of color*

87. Clemensa, a slave

88. Tingo, a slave

89. Iverson, a slave

90. Julian, a slave

91. Bosquet Shorter, a free man of color

92. Betsia, a free woman

93. Thomas, a slave

94. Avarilla, a slave

95. Chaney, a slave

96. Binkey, a slave

97. Rosana Freeland, a free woman

98. Memory Devine, a free man of color

99. Gift Johnson, a free man of color

100. Mahaly, a slave

101. Zedakiah Dorsey, a freed black

102. Bronaugh, a slave

103. Calvert, a slave

March 25, 1983

Beloved,

It's been several hours since I first read your letter. I wish I could be there with you. I hate that I couldn't be at the sentencing. I've felt guilty about not even having time to talk with your lawyer since the 17th. I 'm grateful that you understand how difficult it's been, David.

Why didn't you tell me about your history with Delahaney? I'm not the marshmallow you think I am. I would rather have anticipated bad news than to be smacked like this. I just can't get over it. Thirty years, David. I'm certain we can appeal the sentence. It has to fall under cruel and unusual punishment. It was Spence that pulled the trigger not you and he's already paid the price. I just don't understand how you could be given 30 years for driving the car.

A letter also came from your lawyer. Mr. Nichols gave me your address. You should find a copy of his letter enclosed. I'll call him and find out what our next step should be. Maybe there are some trial matters that can also be appealed. I have the notes you made and the ones I took. I'll send a copy to Nichols. I know there must be something we can do.

Momma is much improved and is back home now. She told me to give you her best. Daddy, too. I spoke to them briefly this evening. I didn't get a chance to tell them about your sentence. The doctors say she has to take it real easy. My Dad's going to have to sit on her to get her to stay put. She's already talking about getting back to her classes. She seems to believe she's the only one who can teach trigonometry. She pouts if the word substitute is uttered.

I went to the hospital with Daddy to pick her up yesterday and she was very frightened being in the car. Even though Daddy is a very safe driver, she was holding on to the dashboard the whole way. She almost put her foot through the floor, trying to brake for Daddy. We all laughed. We're lucky she's alive. The man who struck her was in a '74 Continental. By the looks of her car you would've thought she'd been hit by a steam roller.

I know you didn't mean the things you said. You didn't have to apologize.

We have left messages for George at his base but we haven't actually heard from him since the first part of February. He wrote to say he was going on maneuvers until the end of May. Did I tell you that already? I'm just going on and on without saying very much. I'm sorry, Baby. I guess I'm still stunned by the news.

I'll call the prison in the morning. I'll talk to your Dad and Cedrick as soon as I can. Cat and I seem to be cool. I'll see about getting books to you, too.

I miss you terribly. Your letter was in my mailbox when I got home from work. I almost ripped it trying to open the envelope. Letters from you are real close to sex. I get aroused, no matter what news there is to tell. I can hear your voice as I read your words. You know it's always been your voice that's turned me on. Not that I mind the other parts of you. I've been listening to Johnny Hartman and Elaine Brown all evening. I sat in your closet for a while just smelling your smell and wishing we had gone to my parents for Thanksgiving.

You're stuck with me, I hope you know.

Thinking of you with all my love,
Royce

You would've laughed at me lost in all that green
Green like nothing you ever raised
Green like the golf courses in Richmond
shot up with dye and miracle gro
New Money Traffic Light Glow-In-The-Dark
Lock Up David Lee   Green
I used to see you in the mine
fields mind fields my fields
turning away and spitting as I
tried to blink that Delta color into shades I knew
Mama's jade plant in the living room
the dogwood that marks the reach of our land
Cedrick's truck leaning to the left full of sod
My blinking eyes watered   you would have whooped
and hollered as I have at you
Oh Daddy you would have laughed   I did
to know how much I wanted your juniper hands in mine.

Camille

the name I never called her

she has never asked why

Camille

the name that embraces more beauty

than I dare voice

my tongue dirties what I speak of

Camille

claim me

redeem me

make me who I pretend to be

it's already too late

Tuesday, April 12, 1983
1:13 p.m.
Accommodations, for the next 30 years
The Commonwealth of Virginia

R.C.—

If we're going to make it, your letters cannot take three weeks to reach me. There is too much to do. Since you cannot accept phone calls from me at the library, i would strongly urge you to take measures to ensure a more speedy arrival of my mail. Please call the warden and complain about the length of time it has taken for me to get your letter. i had also expected to receive my materials by now. i have somehow managed to maintain control of my typewriter but i am down to my last six sheets of typing paper. i had also expected you to establish an account at the commissary by now. What is taking you so long, Royce? Cat wrote and said she has not heard from you. Please do not aggravate me, Royce. i cannot contain all of this here. i expect an explanation asap.

David

P.S. Be more precise in noting the date and hour of your letter. It was difficult to understand when you received the letter. Today is not the same as yesterday. You know me well enough to do better!

And i didn't appreciate that little wistful bullshit about going to your parents' house for Thanksgiving. You can sit there in the goddamned closet (what the hell are you doing sitting in the closet, anyway?) and what-if all you want. Did you ever stop to think i didn't choose this? It chose me. And if it hadn't been November 24, 1982—Martinsville, Virginia, it would've been anytime, Anyplace, USA. You hear what i'm saying?!? Cut that "if only" shit out. If you're going to listen to Elaine Brown, then fucking listen to the lyrics.

This is not my fault. This is **not my** fault. This is **not my**
fault **This.**

I don't believe this is what I meant for myself.

Not after Royce

after Bluefields

Oakland

L.A.

Santa Fe

Da Nang

Manila

Royce Not after

Royce

could I choose this

these outskirts this border town No.

No more than I chose

my platoon

my place of birth

the So-Lo Gas Station

an almost son

or Spence

No.

I am one of the chosen people.

Mama let me stay with you
let me sit with you
wash your feet in turpentine and milk
I prayed three days and nights
just like you taught me
my hands open
my forehead to the ground
I recited Scripture
and listened to the candles talk in my mind
but still I'm bound here
let me touch the dark earth where you are
let me smell your tobacco body
it's been so long.

Got my twist and shout ready
Ain't seen a player like me yet
Gonna low stroke through my thirty
Like a viper through brome grass

They gonna wonder nightly
How to contuse my wild black ass

How to break me into pieces
Put my mind into a trance

But I've got something for them
My hoodoo agitation dance
Gonna sweat like Bruh Sisyphus
Rocking steady til my last.

New fish in the tank:
I could've sworn I was on the Mekong
the call of numbers
the way the column was moving
the weight of chains
the weight of gear
that same slow motion lift of the shoulders
men pulling themselves out of the mud and forward
with their shoulders
their bodies twitching from strain
tongues flicking
sweat maps on their backs
heads carried the same way
careful deliberate rotations checking for snipers

foolish jerking moves that proclaim willingness and fear
the uniform and shoes feel the same
they are not mine but I had better make them mine
pray over the threads and leather so I won't go down
the old recruits look the same
their eyes searching for a fuck
searching for a friend
searching for relief
searching for distraction from the
boredom of survival.

My body confuses them for now. I have put explosives in my eyes. They see detonation and pieces flying, catching them in critical places. I have hardened the line of my jaw and I clench my teeth. In the pulse of working muscles, they can read, "All bets are off." My hands and back still show field work. They think I have been on the chain. Thanks, Daddy. They speak and I turn slowly like I'm about to unleash myself but not so slowly that I tax their patience or their interest. I tap all the vocabularies that I know, choose wisely, say little.

They know about my 30 years. They think I have killed. That's good.

I have been watching The Fruit. I let them see me pray on my knees, facing East, My arms open. It is not a lie. This is how I pray. But I do let them see into me. I exchange the proper greetings, salutations, nods. They read my intensity as faith.

They read my detachment as devotion. I will have to declare myself soon. I will need to get a Koran. Declare myself. I wonder what will happen if I do. Declarations get me in trouble. Declaring myself with Royce. Declaring myself with Spence. Perhaps it is not the declaration but the independence I have trouble with. Shit, if only I could put this quick wit to purpose.

Perhaps it is something I could do. If nothing else, for the shade of their tree.

Mama—

Thank you for watching over me.

Thank you for keeping me safe.

Thank you for the blessing of this single cell.

Thank you for the hot water on my body.

Thank you for the sun on my face.

Thank you for the letter from Catherine and the pictures of Baby Lee.

Thank you for time away from the smell of despair.

Please let me hear from Royce.

Please let me hear from Daddy and Cedrick.

For your love, guidance, and protection I am most grateful.

Mama? Is my son with you?

I hate your letters. They are not you. They are not bridge but canyon. I cannot speak across them. My voice echoes and returns to me hollow. They are not door. Not window. They are rope twisted around my neck. They are me dangling

Camille

I would write all day and night of you and release who I am in my words. I would confide my desire to float in you. And then what? I cannot touch you. My hands have been made into paws.

If I loved you, I would leave you shredded. Adored but mangled.

Let me touch you.

Please don't write me. Don't ever stop. Don't write me.

Don't ever stop.

(Rewind)

You are kissing your woman good-bye. She does not want you to go. She is putting electricity into her kisses. She tastes as she did 11 years ago. Like cool water. She is pressing her stomach against you. She is holding onto your arms like you are the keeper of all of her secrets. You are holding onto her with fear. Still, she is cool water. Why do you want to go? Why are you afraid? You stop kissing first. You move your right hand from her hip and take her right hand from your left arm. You break the connection. You pretend you have done this so you can kiss her hand. Her hand smells of roses and you kiss it with more of you than you intended. The heart of her hand is soft. It arouses you. Why do you want to go? You look in her eyes and know it is true. You love this woman. Why are you afraid? You want this woman. A part of you believes if you stay you will die. A part of you believes if you leave you will die. You embrace her to keep from dying. Fuck, she is melting into you. The voice that wants to go speaks loudly and you leave. You are driving south and your thoughts are of her. The her she is, the her you are afraid she might be. The her she is when you are not with her. The her she is only with you. The her who is daughter, who is sister. The her who will be your wife. Your wife your wife your wife your wife. You watch the white line and know you have crossed it. You watch the line and know it is your father. You watch the line and know it is your life. You watch the line and know it has nothing to do with you. Through the windshield you see scenes from a marriage. You see your mother's grave. You see Royce in a casket. You are running off the road. You are crying. You see things clearly now.

April 19, 1983
Mr. Carmichael :

The only reason I'm writing this letter is because David wants me to and it's hard for me to say no to David, especially now. If I never saw you or Cedrick again it would be too soon. I can't imagine how Catherine managed to live with you as long as she did, you bastards. I can only imagine that Mrs. Carmichael was relieved the day she died. I'll never tell about the shed, Cedrick's filthy hands, you watching and smiling and waiting to tell Cedrick to get off of me. I'll never mention how Cedrick laughed when I started to cry. I'll never say because David already knows who you are. Confirmation would only re-open a slow-healing wound.

Go to hell, motherfucker and take your sorry-ass son with you.

Duty done,

C. R. Dumas

(Rewind - flip).
You are kissing your man good-bye. He wants to go. He is dulling his kisses. He tastes disconnected like he did 11 years ago. Like warm water from a tin cup. He is pulling from you. He is holding onto to you fearfully. Why do you want him to stay? He stops kissing first. He moves his right hand from your hip and takes your right hand from his left arm. He breaks the connection. He pretends he has done this so he can kiss your hand. You know this. You know more than he wants you to know about him. Your hand smells of roses and it arouses him. He looks in your eyes and knows you know the truth. He holds you like he is dying. You melt into him to save his life. He leaves. He is driving south. Taking parts of you with him. He watches the white line and thinks it is the glue that keeps the world from opening up. He is crying. He wipes his eyes. He sees something that he did not see before. There is no escape.

April 20, 1983
Dear David,
You may have forgotten, but fourteen years ago, I told you if you ever hit me again, I would never speak to you. As far as I'm concerned your last letter was a TKO.
Do I write you to say that I'm never going to speak to you again?

April 20, 1983
Dear David,
What do you want from me? Please, just tell me. It will make it easier on both of us.

April 20, 1983
David,
Be patient, my love. I know, that's easier said than done. Things are going to work out. Daddy would say, "When pigs fly."

April 21, 1983
David,
Fuck you! Why is it you can really piss me off and I think about making love to you? There may be sickness here. I don't know why I'm laughing.

April 21, 1983
Dearest David,
I'm sorry that I didn't take care of things the way you wanted me to.
There must be words that will calm you down but not make me . . .

April 21, 1983
Dear David,
Someone wrote me a letter and signed your name. He is a real asshole. Do you know who he is? I can't figure it out. That's pretty awful.

April 21, 1983
Beloved,
There's something I've been meaning to tell you about your father and Cedrick. Remember the day you went to Roanoke? Cedrick thought it would be fun to measure himself in me. Your father thought it would be fun to let him try. God only knows what stopped them both.
You don't deserve that.

April 27, 1983

Dear Mr. Carmichael
Dear Cedrick,

I hope this finds both of you in good health and business going well. Please forgive the delay in my writing to you. My mother was hospitalized after an automobile accident. She is home now and doing better but it continues to be a bit hectic here. As you know, I have not been well myself. I deeply regret not being with you at David Lee's sentencing.

You must have been devastated having to hear that terrible sentence in the courtroom. I have told Mr. Nichols that I will do everything in my power to get David Lee a new trial, and barring that, to get his sentence reduced. I thought I might write to some of David Lee's acquaintances and teachers asking for letters of support in this effort. I remember meeting a Mrs. Scott one time when David and I were in the IGA in Martinsville. She was David Lee's 11th grade English teacher. I remember her saying how brilliant David Lee was and how wonderful the letters were that he wrote from Viet Nam. She was so generous with her praise, she made David Lee blush. Please let me know how I might get in touch with her and any other people you think might be of help. Also, please let me know if there is anything I might do to make it easier for you. I love David Lee very much. Very, very much.

If you and I have had problems in the past, please accept my apologies. I know that sometimes I have allowed my love for David Lee to make me impatient and insensitive to what you must be experiencing. I do so much want for us to be a family. Please let me earn your trust and love. I hope to get to Virginia very soon.

With my very best wishes.

Warmly,
Camille Royce

Thursday April 21, 1983
7:05:32 p.m.

Dear Mr. Carmichael,

1) I received your April 12 letter today at 5:47 p.m.

2) I received your letter of Thursday, March 17 on Thursday, March 24. I wrote to you shortly after midnight on Friday, March 25. Please ascribe any ambiguities in my letter regarding time and date to my feelings of disappointment and anguish.

3) Warden Cristfield relates: "Inmates who experience initial difficulties with their mail, normally find that after 90 days, correspondence and packages are received in a more timely manner."

4) A commissary account has been opened in your name/id# in the amount of $100.00 (your monthly limit for the next 6 months).

5) After explaining to Warden Cristfield that you are continuing your education through correspondence, he okayed the direct mailing of office supplies from Ginn's Office Supply to you on a quarterly basis upon receipt of copies of documents verifying your affiliation with Antioch. Such materials have been sent: receipts of registration, transcripts, notice of good standing.

6) Enclosed find a copy of a letter addressed to Michael Turblo Carmichael and Cedrick Michael Carmichael,

7) I have been studying Elaine Brown's lyrics to better understand the political aspects of your fate.

8) I didn't know armed robbery was freedom fighting.

9) From now on, I will keep my fantasies to myself.

10) From now on, I will keep my secrets to myself.

11) From now on, I will keep my love to myself.

12) I can't wait for my next task.

13) This letter will be mailed at the main post office, Washington, D.C. before 8:30 p.m.)

14) No #14, I just didn't want to end on #13.

C. Royce Dumas

[letter completed Thursday, April 21, 1983 at 7:29:36]

April 28, 1983

Dear Mr. Carmichael and Cedrick,

I hope the business is doing well. I'm sorry I wasn't able to write sooner. I'm also sorry that I was unable to be with you at David Lee's sentencing. My mother was hospitalized after an automobile accident. She is home now and doing better but it continues to be a bit hectic here.

I have told Mr. Nichols that I will do everything in my power to get David Lee a new trial, and barring that, to get his sentence reduced. I thought I might write to some of David Lee's acquaintances and teachers asking for letters of support in this effort. I remember meeting a Mrs. Scott one time when David and I were in the IGA in Martinsville. She was David Lee's 11th grade English teacher. I remember her saying how brilliant David Lee was and how wonderful the letters were that he wrote from Viet Nam. She was so generous with her praise! Please let me know how I might get in touch with her and any other people you think might be of help.

I love David Lee very much. I hope to get to Virginia very soon.

With my very best wishes.

Warmly,
Camille Royce

Monday, May 9, 1983
2:32 p.m.
Virginia Correctional Facility
Richmond, Virginia
Dearest Royce—

Thank you, Baby, for taking care of everything. i got my materials along with your letter this morning. Your note to my family was beautiful and gracious, as you are. i especially liked the part about my brilliance. i know you don't like them, Royce. i'm not sure i like them. But they are my family.

By the way, Daddy and Cedrick weren't able to get to the sentencing. Don't worry. i've written to tell them you didn't know so they won't misread your comment about their courtroom devastation as some kind of roundabout insult. i love you. Forgive me for the cruelty of my last letter. i see Nichols tomorrow about appeal work. i can't wait to see you. When are you coming? Please don't write me anymore letters like the last one. i can't stand it when you're angry with me. i think you are wonderful. Have i told you lately?

Devotedly,
David

P.S. We could debate the politics of armed robbery. But i will leave that for another letter. i would only say, and this is not an excuse, that the world is turned upside down, Royce, and often it's difficult to know what's good and what's bad and why people do what they do. For good, for harm. *The world is turned upside down and were it not for you, i would fly right off into space. Take care, my love.*

Saturday, May 14, 1983
3:55 p.m.

Dearest David,

When you get angry with me, it makes me feel like you don't understand how much I love you and that I'm in your corner for real. And then I get mad at myself for getting mad at you for being mad at me. It gets funky real fast. I do understand what you say about this world. Sometimes I feel like we're on a roller coaster that goes upside down and backwards and we can't get off. And I'd really like to get off. Anyway, I'm glad you got everything and were satisfied with the letter to your family.

I've called Cat a couple of times and she's doing really well. She says that when the baby is a few months older, she'll come see you in Richmond. It's a long drive and Dennis doesn't want her to go alone. His mom doesn't think a prison is the right place for a newborn. Cat told Dennis his mother could kiss her ass. She says to tell you don't worry she'll be there and she wants to know if you liked the pictures of the baby.

I thought I might try to get to Richmond for Memorial Day weekend. I was going to surprise you but I realized there isn't much time and that you might not have put me on your visitors list yet. David, my funds are a little short, so please don't bombard me with a list of a thousand things to bring.

How does letter sex strike you? More on this and other subjects later. Daddy just called and asked me to come by the house as soon as I could. I'm going to try to get this over to the post office on my way to see my folks. Hopefully, everything is okay over there. I'll keep my toes and fingers crossed and hope you get this before the 27th of May.

You know all this stuff, David: who's the patron saint of grass widows?

How about letter-writing grass widows?

Much love and many kisses,
Royce

104. Topsail Fauntleroy, a freed black

105. Guttridge, a slave

106. Solomon Carpenter, a freed black

107. Cloey, a slave

108. Jiney Pendleton, a free man of color

109. Diadama, a slave

110. Tade, a slave

111. Mahitable James, a free woman of color

112. Kissey Fortune, a freed black

113. Sovereign World, a freed black

114. Saphronia, a slave

115. Temperance, a slave

116. Negro Milly, a free woman of color

117. Lazarus Cooper, a freed black

118. Esther Queen, a slave

119. Ezpearance, a slave

120. Fortunatus Brisco, a freed black

121. Polydore, a free man of color

122. Onando, a free man of color

123. Willy Ricks, a free man of color

124. Caroline, a slave

125. Amity, a slave

126. Abergail, a slave

127. Gabe, a slave

128. Ramsey Boston, a freed black

129. Thomas Commodore, a freed black

130. Plato Greenwell, a freed black

131. Gardiner Harrison, a freed black

132. Butterfield, a slave

133. Phoebe, a slave

134. Obedience, a slave

135. Trusilla Cummings, a freed black

136. Notice, a slave

137. Ruth Collins, a free woman of color

138. Abah Whitley

139. Carie Dennison

140. Essex Messenger, a freed black

141. Bess, a slave

142. Kauchee, a slave

. . . Ah jes wanna leave dis one thought wid you, Proverbs 25:25. "As cold waters to a thirsty soul, so is good news from a far country." In Cross Keys, we pleny scared. We scared den. We scared now. But we was real parched and Prophet Nat turned hisself into our far country. In Southampton County, May rains still taste sweeter. Dat's God's truth. Ah lak to think dat somewheres in de Great Dismal, de water cold and sweet, too. Ah got people in dere.

. . . Man, there were hundreds of names on those damn lists. We must've done eight or nine a day and we didn't make a dent. But what choice was there? Funeral detail or riot duty. Hell, if that was a choice, I sure didn't feel like I was choosing. They paired me up with Reggie Nance who lost part of his right arm and his right leg. They thought that would make the families feel sorry for us and not try to kill the messengers, so to speak. Shit, those mothers beat the hell out of my chest. Fathers just sat there glassy-eyed and limp. I can hear myself sitting down on those plastic slipcovers, looking at the little candy dishes on the coffee tables and the high school graduation pictures on the TV sets. I didn't want to look into the people's eyes. Each morning for 14 weeks, Reggie and I called out the day's names, planned our little chats with the families, mapped out our routes through the city, and tried not to slide back into Nam. But what choice was there? You know, there was this brother at the VA—Thompkins was his name. He had this tattoo that covered most of his chest. Said he got it in Phan Thiet. A big pierced heart and the words "We are buried with him by baptism into death." Yeah.

Do I tell you of this coffin space? Do I need to?
When you closet-sit smelling me are you already here
in this closeness
the gunpowder and dogs up in our noses
the odors trifling with our brains
and memories?
In here the past is present
We can never speak of what is now
It doesn't exist between us
There is only remember when
remember that time
remember her
remember him
remember me
In this place
each letter is nostalgia
each letter is a tunnel dark on either end
What can I tell you
that you won't already know
by the time I speak it?

Since you were 12 and I 14, I have wanted you. Not in the way that preoccupies us here. Not the amphibian sex that makes us think we can take off and land wherever we want. Not the violent push into another world that makes us think being brutal is the same as being. No. I have not craved you in those ways. I have wanted you as confirmation

evidence

proof

of me.

I have wanted to bury myself in you and have you as my tombstone. Have I gotten my wish?

Please, say yes.

Please, never answer this.

I can never write these things. Never write them. Never write them. Never. Write. Them. I can only carry them around with me. Ball bearings. I can see my head tilting and little balls plinking out onto the concrete floor. Rolling . . . rolling. Slipping under the bars. Falling through the cat walk. Raining on someone else's head. Opening up his skull. Joining with more unspeakable, unwritable, fevered things. That has a nice symmetry to it.

Dear Cedrick,

You have not written. You have not come to see me. You don't give a fuck. Sibling of mine.

You might even be happier with me here, Big Brother. Did I say might? Now you can hit on Royce straight up. No more little bullshit flirtations. No more lame ass games. No more needing to act like you was just being friendly. I have told her to kill you if she has to. I wonder if that would turn you on.

Yeah, you're the golden boy, now. You don't have to work at tossing out no more guilt trips. How you the only one ever stayed with Daddy. How you the one who buried Mama. How you the one who lost three fingers bush hogging. How you the one never had a chance for college. How you the one don't know all those hifalutin motherfucking words. How you the one fought the battle of Martinsville, Virginia—didn't have to go to no Viet Nam. How you the one never had the luxury to gallivant all around the world. How you the one never had a woman like Royce. How you the one! How you the one! How you the one!

You gonna be in heaven now, Cedrick. For the next thirty years you got a built-in excuse why you don't ever have to do shit. You have secured your position as number one son, Cedrick. You might even finally convince Daddy to change the name of the business to Carmichael & Son.

A simple thank you would suffice.

Royce,

I've tried hard not to ask you this. I've tried to believe the little you have told me. I know if ever I write my questions down, or speak them aloud, you will leave me. But it is either your fault or it is mine. I need to know. I can forgive you.

Perhaps three months ago, the possibility that I would be exactly where I am scared you. In fact, it scared you so badly that you found someone to take out the part of me you carried. This is Cedrick's line—that the stupidity of my actions made you get rid of it. This is my father's line, also. You and I are both bad farmers in Daddy's eyes. I am particularly so because I have the knack for growing, I just won't use it. I don't know why I care what they think. As much as I hate them, I love them. God, help us.

Being here makes it impossible to judge you. But I do it without ceasing. When I saw you at the courthouse in that old blue coat, you looked 16, again. Your hands were icy and when I reached inside your coat, your stomach was round and very warm. When I touched it, I thought something must be in there making it hot. When I touched it, I wanted someone to touch me back. Your eyes said, "Please, don't touch me there."

Cedrick says you are a good actress but Cedrick wants you for himself or maybe he just doesn't want me to have you. I don't really believe you have lied. I do consider the possibility that you have not told me the truth.

All I have is your letter. Or rather, I used to have your letter. I learned of him and his passing at the same time. "I was pregnant." "Was pregnant?" I said aloud. The men around me stared. One of the guards laughed and I wanted to knock the shit out of him. I carried that letter with me until the day of the sentencing. I tore it into little pieces. I liked tearing it up. I held on to the pieces all day. No matter what. As I was boarding the bus, my waist chained and hands cuffed, I let go of those bits of you, hoping the March air would take them away. Instead they fell to the ground. Some fluttered into puddles of oil and the previous day's rain. Royce, I came so close to breaking then. Me on the edge of 30 years, those soiled pieces, and a dead baby were too much. They're still too much.

Why didn't you tell me before I left? Is that why you were anxious for me to stay? I wonder if that was why I was so anxious to go.

I wanted to ask you on that last day we were together. We both just had too much to explain. As I waited for you to tell me about your body, you waited for me to tell you about my crime.

I thought you were the criminal. Cedrick and my Dad had been pressing their views hard. They made me feel like a fool. I don't know why I couldn't ignore them.

I halfway wish I could tell you I woke up that morning thinking what a good idea it would be to rob a convenience store. But running into Spence was an accident. I still can't explain why I took the gun he offered. And I can't begin to tell you what I felt, my face in the gravel, a foot on my back, another on my neck, guns pointed at my head, and Spence ten feet away, spread eagle on the ground and painted red.

I wish you could tell me something.

Royce, I dream of my son. Not that I know it was a boy. Was it a boy? Some nights I dream that he is dangling from a cliff and I can't hold him. As small as he is, I can't hold on. Some nights I dream I let him go and watch him drop. I watch his small arms wave bye-bye. Some nights you are smiling at his grave. Some nights he is smiling at yours. Some nights I can't see your face at all but hear you crying. Royce, I dream almost every night of David Lesesne Carmichael, Jr. My boy. Our child. What do you dream?

It's a blessing that he's gone. It breaks my heart.

Mama, tell me.

I know you know.

Did you say something to Royce? Whisper in her ear?

Did you say something to my son? Coax him with the pleasures of death?

Did you lean on Royce's stomach and press him out?

Did you say, no more Carmichael men?

I wouldn't blame you, Mama.

I dreamed Royce's stomach was a lens

and that baby looked through

and saw his Daddy's people up close

and said, no way.

No way at all.

David, you doing some serious dredging today. Why does it all have to come together like some kind of nasty stew? You the one talking about a death being a blessing. Don't lay that at my feet!

She was thinkin she was free instead of jes runaway. Her whole life actin like there was a safe place jes on the other side. A place where she be God's chile. We done cry for her. Jes like we done cry for our own selves.

Sunday, May 15, 1983
morning time

Dearest David,

I am burning Nag Champa. The apartment smells sanctified. Eric Dolphy is on the box. "It's Magic." The neighbors are going to get sick of hearing it. I am leaning against the couch as I write and the sunlight through the window is warming my toes. I've put on some coffee. I just want the aroma. I can see you bringing your coffee cup to your lips but setting it down to cuss about something in the Sunday *Post*. I can think about these things and believe you will be back.

I was up at the playground this morning, sliding down the spiral like we used to. I could feel your arms around me, your chin on my shoulder, your lips against my ear. I climbed your tree and watched the sun come up over the cemetery.

I am wearing clothes you bought for me. Do you remember the lemon yellow blouse you got in Viet Nam? The one with the little pleats and lace and the ribbon running through the collar? And the turquoise skirt from New Mexico? It's easeful. I love to twirl in it. These are the clothes I wear in my dreams of you, when I am wearing clothes. I am bathed, oiled, smelling of lavender, and dressed for you. I feel strong this morning, David. I wonder if it is because you are well. I hope it is because you are well. I feel like a dancer in the movies, ready to leap into your arms. I feel beautiful in all the things you have given me.

I used to wonder about your plans for me. It seems like you had plans from the start. I think if my parents hadn't known your family, they would never have allowed me to keep your presents. You never wrote a letter. You just sent these wonderful packages with a little card saying where the gift was from. I always thought the way you signed the cards was funny. Your Friend—David Lesesne Carmichael. I still have all of those cards, you know. So David Lesesne Carmichael, my friend, what were you plotting? The bag from Guatemala. The earrings from the Philippines. The silver bracelets from Guadalajara (I wear them everyday to work). What was the plan?

As long as we have known each other, you have never said. Have you loved me as long as I've loved you? Did you know you could seduce me with mementos of your adventures? Could you see who I was before I could see myself? There were nine years of gifts before you kissed me, unless you count that terrible, exciting kiss when I was 12. You talk about not knowing what's good or bad but I have always thought you and I were good. I've always thought you were good, David. And I don't think I've ever told you that. There have been times when you were sleeping with your head on my lap that you looked like an angel. Not perfect, mind you, but an angel nonetheless. I know there must be an important reason why you got involved with the robbery.

I woke up this morning thinking I really hadn't written you a letter. There has been business correspondence but no real letter. It's kind of strange but time seems more critical now and I want to try and say as much as I can to you. I haven't seen you since February 9 at 4:05 when you said everything was going to be okay. So much change in three months and there is so much we haven't said. Can we say it? I wonder, David, what can we write to one another? All the things I've said so far, can I really say them? Can I start to tell you what I've needed to say? Can we talk of love and making love with countless eyes on the page? What language is there for us that is private?

The envelope of your last letter was stamped:

Received VCF - Mailroom. The Department of Corrections Has Neither Censored Nor Inspected This Item. Therefore The Department Does Not Assume Responsibility For Its Contents.

Does that mean they inspect and censor mail but just not your particular letter?

You know what, I don't care. I mean I care about you being safe, but I don't care about who knows how I feel about you and how long I've felt that way. I really don't care. If I start to worry about who reads this other than you, it's over. I won't be able to say anything because everything that is me, is full of you.

Yesterday, I went over to Taylor Street . My father summoned me. I was afraid that my mom had had some kind of relapse but it turned out they were having an anniversary party. She was unconscious on March 13. Needless to say, they didn't have a chance to celebrate their 30th year together.

The three of us stood around a beautiful cake, all silver and white with bells and fondant pearls. I wish George had been there. Can't you just see him in his Dodgers cap and McKinley sweatshirt? Do you remember when we double dated with him and Consuela, the nurse over at Providence Hospital? We went to the movies. It was really bad but I don't think George or Consuela saw much of it. It's a funny thing, David, I can't even remember what we saw, just that it was awful and that you and George picked it. Actually, I think Consuela and I did.

Anyway, you should have seen Daddy. He was adorable. He pulled out this huge box. David, it must have been three feet wide. Momma's smile was enormous. I've never seen her smile like that. Don't you know the box was wrapped in beautiful lilac paper with a big royal purple bow and a bunch of silk violets tucked under the bow. You know Momma loves purple. She had such a time opening that box. She can't really stand up long yet so she had trouble getting at it. We put it on the floor but that was too low. I cleared off the dining room table and that was too high. Then I sat with the box on my lap while she tugged at the tape on the paper and then the corners of the box. The box was full of purple tissue paper. Finally, she got to another box, a shoe box. And that box was wrapped like the big box had been. She held that shoe box in her lap for the longest time. Just held it. And then she took off the ribbon and the paper and opened the box. Inside was another box. A wooden box in the shape of a heart. It was lacquered like the Chinese do. My dad had made it for her. She took the top off carefully. The inside of the box was lined and smelled like the potpourri Momma keeps in the ginger jar next to the record cabinet. And there was a tiny purple box in the center of the heart. Daddy ran to the stereo and put on Dinah Washington singing, "You Go to My Head." Then he nodded that it was okay for her to open the little box. Momma cradled the box in her hands and lifted the lid. There was a pair of gold earrings in the shape of love knots. Daddy had made those, too, with the help of Mr. Jacobs' son who is a dental student at Howard. You remember Mr. Jacobs? He was the one who gave us that bushel of peaches. Remember? Momma and Daddy both started crying and I felt jubilant for them. I want us to be like them. David, I felt like I was the one who'd been given a gift. It sounds silly but it made me feel like all things were possible. That you and I are possible. That love is possible. I know what you're saying, don't get all carried away and sappy.

Anyway, I stayed at Mom and Dad's long after they went to bed. They went to bed very early and I could hear them giggling all the way out in the living room. I don't know what they were doing with Momma still weak. Daddy came out to check on me about 12:30 and asked me if I wanted to stay over. He also reminded me about Mother's Day. Honestly, it made me feel dizzy. I let out a little cry. I surprised myself, David. He asked me what was wrong. He put his arm around me. He looked right at me and said, "I like that boy, Camille. He's mighty intense and he can butt with a billy goat but I like him." Can you believe it? It must be magic.

Thinking about you has helped this day pass. I do wish I was looking down at a watermelon stomach. I'll give your sister a call tonight.

With all my heart,
Royce

There is no place to weep or grieve
No room for penance on my terms
For retribution on theirs
There is nothing between my legs
And all around me
Brothers work nonexistent dicks
Trying to extract life

Someone should tell them

Tell them what?

April 1, 1983

Hey, Fool—

What's shaking, Sis? Thought I'd drop you a line on your birthday. Get it? April Fools? Your birthday? Anyway, how you and that fool man of yours doing? When are you guys jumping the broom? I need to get it straight so I can apply for leave. My CO is pretty straight dealing and he's got a baby sister so I figure I'll be there.

How's Mom and Pop? I called the hospital a couple of days ago and they said she had been released. How come nobody's ever home when I call? I assume no news is good news. You can write me in care of Edwards and I'll get the letter eventually. Has Pop stopped smoking yet? Tell him he better. Tell him I bowled a 274 at the base. He better put some ju-ju on his ugly ass ball or his first born is going to kick his butt. I know you won't mind if Pop and I miss your wedding rehearsal to get a few games in over at Fair Lanes.

Got to go. Tell David to stay the fuck out of trouble until I get there.

Stay loose, Cammy.

Brother George

Monday, May 16, 1983
1:10 a.m.

David,

Sometimes, most times I wonder what put us together to be apart. It's a cruel thing. At the same time that it's a sweet thing. Sometimes I think I'm crazy because our separation makes my love for you so intense. It's like the edge of orgasm all the time. I don't mean physically. But that rush— of wondering when we'll be together again—feels really good. I can taste it. Actually taste it. I have to stop myself. I don't want pain to be pleasurable. I don't want a romance novel of a life. I want you. But it's hard not to get lost in the fantasies that swirl around me. I'm afraid I'm not making sense. I guess I want to ask you, how does it feel to you . . . Apart from me? Is it all pain? Do you allow yourself the pleasure of it? Does each letter seem like foreplay or like a grenade?

Royce

P.S. I got a letter from George today. I want you to know, mail is stranger in the service than it is in prison. He wrote me April 1. That's six weeks. But then again, he didn't say when he mailed it and I couldn't read the postmark. He used to sign his letters "The Road Runner." He loved those cartoons. Now he signs "Brother George" like I'm supposed to be impressed by my big brother's words. I miss him. Anyway, he said to tell you hello and to stay loose.

Monday, May 16, 1983
11:02 p.m.

Beloved,

Today was a good day at the Library. Usually Thursdays are hard because they are so long. Baderinwa is out on maternity leave and I took over her evening slot. I was working on a display case on poetry. It's about poetry around the world. Senghor, Luis Morales, Antonio Neto. Okot P'Bitek. Murilo Mendes. Kofi Awoonor. Tchicaya U Tam'si. Dennis Brutus. Rene Depestre. Mazisi Kunene. Derek Walcott. Your favorites. I haven't got a title yet. So far all I can come up with is "Around the World in Poetry." Pretty tired, right? I'm still trying to track down some collections by women poets outside the U.S. I should have at least a couple of women, don't you think?

I was flipping through *Los versos del Capitán*. Pablo Neruda. It's been such a long time since I've read those poems. It was like I had never read them. I guess the last time I read them was before you and I were really together. I know, I know. We've always been together. I'm talking about together in the same place, same time, on the same wave length together.

How's your Spanish? I ordered you a copy of the verses from Records and Books after I got off. You remember Terence? He's short and very serious looking? He said to tell you hello and he gave me a good deal on the book. I got the one that has the Spanish and English. He let me put bookmarks in it for you before he boxed it up. When you get it, see what you think. Perhaps Neruda can be our private language.

"Your Hands"
"When your hands go out,
love, toward mine,
what do they bring me flying?
Why did they stop
at my mouth, suddenly,
why do I recognize them
as if then, before,
I had touched them,
as if before they existed
they had passed over
my forehead, my waist? . . .

All the years of my life
I walked around looking
for them."

"Tus Manos"
"Cuando tus manos salen,
amor, hacia las mias,
qué me traen volando?
Por qué se detuvieron
en mi boca, de pronto,
por qué las reconozco
como si entonces, antes,
las hubiera tocado,
como si antes de ser
hubieran recorrido
mi frente, mi cintura? . . .

Los años de mi vida
yo caminé buscándolas."

Always,
Royce

P. S. Sorry for such a pedestrian postscript. I know you have other things on your mind, but if you come up with a good title for my display case, let me know. If you feel like it, we can talk about it when I see you.

A man named Chester calls himself Pearl. Fancies himself with large breasts and magnificent hips. He works his show. Works full-time. I look at him with disdain. Curiosity, sympathy, desire would be too costly. I want to ask him, "What the hell are you doing?" I want to ask him, "What does this mean to you?" I want to ask him, "Do you get what you want?" I want to ask him, "Can you ever go back to being someone else?" But the hint of any of these questions on my lips would bring, "You know you want it" to his. It is not the sex I'm interested in, although I question why I think about Pearl so much. I believe I want Chester's answers. I believe they are curled up tight with my own.

Monday, May 23, 1983
5:19 p.m.
Virginia Correctional Facility
Richmond, Virginia

Baby—
Got your May 15th letter this morning. Yes, of course, you are on my list! Everything is set. Good news from Nichols. He believes there are many appeal possibilities. He is working on the brief. i haven't felt this good in weeks. You coming. Nichols' enthusiasm. Catherine sent me more pictures of Lee. She said she named her after me although Dennis doesn't know it. Today, i can even be genuinely happy about Cat's new baby. There are so many things I want but nothing more than you. i don't know the regulations about food. Can you check? R.C., some jerk chicken. Baby, please? With pigeon peas and rice. A ginger beer and a potato roti. Oh, hell, there's not enough time.

Nothing more than you. Nothing more.

Love,
David

P.S. Yes, it would make more sense to give you this letter when I see you but this is the closest I can get to talking to you right now. Things are going so well, tell your Mom i might have to go to chapel on Sunday. My first step towards salvation. I can hear her hallelujah already.

P.P.S. One more thing, could you please order me some magazines. It doesn't matter what. The thicker the better. *Playboy*, *GQ*. *Ebony*'s okay but it's too thin sometimes. Save the *Black Enterprise* Top 100 issue for me. Remember, thick magazines.

One more one more thing. Baby, please don't ever call yourself a widow of any kind. I know what you meant, but Royce, the word hurts me.

Wednesday, May 25, 1983
I don't know what time it is
and I don't care

David,

I took my car over to Tony's shop. Everything checked out. I got a tune up and the tires rotated. I washed it this evening for good luck. I'm off from the 27th through the 31st, so I'll be able to see you Friday, Saturday, Sunday, and Monday. I've got reservations at one of the Holiday Inns down there. I'm leaving here as soon as the morning rush hour is over.

I'm assuming you want a roti and peas and rice. Mrs. Higginbotham says she'll have you thinking you were in Kingston. Daddy is going to lend me this chest he has that keeps things hot. Speaking of hot, will I be able to touch you? I meant to ask you earlier. I didn't want to call and ask them that. But it doesn't matter. It doesn't matter at all.

I don't know why I'm writing, you won't get this before I see you. I guess it's just part of trying to share as much as possible with you.

There are a few surprises (good surprises) I'm trying to work out.

I'm so excited, I can hardly write. Be there soon.

Love,
Royce

Thursday, May 26, 1983
10:00 p.m.

David,

Nichols called about an hour ago and told me I shouldn't expect to see you tomorrow. He said you'd been placed in isolation because of an altercation with a guard. I'm not sure what to do now. I don't know if I should come or if coming would make things worse. Nichols said not to bother. Nichols said you'd be in for 90 days. Nichols said the fight started over something in one of my letters. He also said he had something for me from you. I'm not sure what to say now. I didn't mean to do anything stupid. I'll call the prison tomorrow and try to see what's what. I'm sorry, Baby.

Royce

You must have known Terence
would pull my heart up
and leave it lodged in my throat
so I could hardly breathe
You must have known
I would picture you walking towards him
smiling
your hand touching his
a whisper
Neruda's words fluttering from your lips
doves
You must have known
offering a dead Chilean to translate
what we can't speak
would crush my bones
You must have known
you on the page like that

would kill me
or make me kill someone
Where did you learn this torture
this skill of making me ache all the more?

Friday, May 27, 1983
3:07 a.m.

David,

I feel like my tongue's been removed. I'm a stump and someone is counting my rings to see how long I have lived. I feel their fingers pressing on raw and dying nerves.

I feel like I was in the car with my mother, pinned under the steering wheel.

I feel like a suspect. I have not been able to breathe properly since Nichols called. I keep thinking someone is going to burst in. I have put a chair under the door knob. I can never send you this. Can I?

I feel like all of these things and none of these things. I don't feel like anything at all.

I want to go to my mother and have her hold me. I want to go to my father and tell him to hurt someone. Who would I point him to?

Up until now, foolishly stupidly, I mailed everything I wrote to you, as if there were no consequences, as if your sentence didn't really mean curtailment, and interdictions. No wonder you have memorized the dictionary.

I want to go to Momma and have her tell me how you live on life support. What can I write, David? I know you can't answer. Weather reports? Library rumors? D.C. scuttlebutt? Sidewalk stories? Cravings but no desire?

What do I do with this? I wish I knew.

I feel like I'm in a grade B movie. High melodrama. Tragic heroine. Sad ending. I hate this! I mean I hate how I don't know how to feel sometimes. I hate feeling stupid. I hate feeling any of this. I hate not just being able to love like normal people. I want to be my Mom and Dad. I don't want to be. I want to be with you. So, who cares what I want.

I can't send you this.

Royce

one could give up writing
around the world in poetry
distances dichotomize people not platoons
ask those who keep the identical appetite for presence
covering miles of crackling earth
dry as a priest's cough and grieving
the acerbic edge of a persimmon dawn alone

    it's magic

no welcome house on the edge of rocks
ask those who chant all night in the clearing
among the red clover of the desert
chewing the cactus regenerated by tears

    why do i tell myself

ask them who give away obituaries
like the evangelist his thank you jesus
ask them who lie in waiting in the shadow
of the cashew tree

    these things that happen are all really true?

ask them who linger at the graves of godchildren
and study the stink weeds and the widow grasses
distances claim people not bodies
ask those who keep rasping dry as a concrete dawn
chewing miles of okra earth
traveling among the purple-edged cactus
on the brink of shadow

ask those who keep their last graves
freshened by kapok trees
ask those who give away the blue grasses
craving the ocean and my love for you
ask those yellowing among the shadows
craving couching writing rasping
ask those who howl
who are separate from people and bodies
how else can i explain the poor who pause
by the graves at the edge of lanes
ask them who give up their lives
grandchildren
for a moment with a .45 caliber
ask those who know
men of death
ask those who know
one could give up
ask those who know
not people
ask those who know
prisoners
ask those who know
distances
ask those who know
writing
one could give up
ask if
it's magic.

March 17, 1983

Camille Royce Dumas
2913 Summit Place, N.E.
Washington, DC 20002

Dear Camille Dumas:
Enclosed please find a gift from Mr. David Carmichael. He wanted me to make sure that you understood that although I purchased the item for him, it was according to his specifications. Please be assured that the inscription is in his hand. He requested I give you this journal in the event of his placement in isolation, illness, or death. I regret the circumstances of this correspondence.

Sincerely,
Geoffrey Baker Nichols
Attorney-at-Law

Date sent May 26, 1983 GBN
enclosure

GBN/kr

To Camille

Make a place for us here when there is no place.

Make a bridge for us here when there are no bridges.

Make an island for yourself when all else fails.

David

3/17/83

To David and Camille,

"Entre tú y yo se abrió una nueva puerta

[Between you and me a new door opened]

y alguien, sin rostro aún,

[and someone, still faceless]

allí nos esperaba."

[was waiting for us there.]

—Pablo Neruda, 8 de Septiembre

I will make all that I can.

Camille Royce Dumas

May 31, 1983

Camille? This is Janeece. Janeece Lorraine Carmichael. David and Catherine's Mama. You've seen me before. You know my light eyes and dark skin. You look in the mirror and see them. I look in you and see myself. Pleased to meet you.

Camille? What you doing with my son, Baby? This is the long haul. Haven't you noticed? I know you want to think it is a dream. Some horrible, metal tasting dream. Some I'm-so-glad-it-was-a-dream dream. But Sweetie, you awake. You awake and living it. I wish I could tell you, "Go on back to sleep. Get you a few more hours." But you can't fool the clock now. You can't fool yourself and think ten more minutes is an hour or one more hour is a day.

Camille? Don't you worry none about Cedrick. I hate to even say it, but he's a lost cause. He's another woman's natural son. I took him on when he was three years old. And me 16. To this day, I don't know if his mama took off or if she's sleeping somewhere in the ground. I took him on when I got myself tangled up with Big Mike. He said Cedrick's mama died in childbirth. I believe that's true some kind of way. Ain't that the funniest name you ever heard? Michael Carmichael. Sounds like a lopsided somebody. And sure enough. My dear mother always said, "Love is blind, crippled, and mad." And sure enough.

If you feel loving David Lee ain't the easiest thing. It's not. Loving ain't easy. Not here. Not in this ooze.

Camille? You can talk to me if you want to. There's no shame in it. Ask me what you want to know. Baby, ain't nobody else gonna tell you.

143. Sobett Jenkins, a freed black

144. Pagg, a slave

145. Kate Hargrove

146. Qussuba, a slave

147. Mercy Williams

148. Ruth, a slave

149. Floor, a slave

150. Feb Taggatt

151. Present, a slave

152. Minde, a slave

153. Adaline Tiller, a freed black

154. Ulysses Primax

155. Cicely Roos

156. Simbo, a slave

157. Awaan, a slave

158. Graham Ragland

159. Lorrie Chapman

160. Wheel Clement, a free man of color

161. Ventured, a slave

162. Yono Cish, a slave

163. Tiller King, a freed black

164. Quamana, a slave

165. Monk Pinkett, a freed black

166. Jake, a slave

167. Corso Blue

168. Limehouse, a slave

169. Everett Cooke, a free man of color

170. Baines, a slave

171. Abraham Litthcut

172. Willing Cutler, a freed black

173. Arvelia Killens

174. Sadler Washington, a freed black

175. Marie, a slave

176. Joseph, a slave

177. Mildred Laurens, a free woman of color

178. Henery Fletcher, a free man of color

179. Elbert Tyson, a freed black

180. Alyce Paso, a free woman of color

181. Wooster, a slave

182. Rayfield Sharp, a free man of color

183. Adaray Wilson, a free man of color

184. Caleb Mills, a freed black

This darkness doesn't scare me. No darkness can after Quang Tri Province. That sticky, heavy night. When there was no moon. When I had no hands. When I had no eyes. When everything was pitch and the smell of death was strong. No one died that night. But our fears had us in body bags, on choppers, in coffins, in the ground, back home. There was also jasmine in the air. No one else smelled it but me. It was Mama telling me "I'm gone, David Lee."

I have stories I can tell myself to mark the hours. I will know when it is morning. When it is light. Even if there are no sounds outside this darkness, I will know. I will feel the surge of waking, restless bodies through the walls. I will feel them as they work the weights, work the tiers, work themselves. I will know. And I will feel them struggling through the night, calling out, calling. I will know and I will be fine.

I have learned from sitting with men in the dark. With the young, hopeful fishermen in Bluefields. With the old, patient farmers in Four Corners. With the nervous, middle-aged marketeers in Manila. I have learned how to rein myself in. I have learned how to watch circumspectly. I have learned how to sit and wait. I have learned how to let what is going to happen come.

This darkness doesn't scare me. No darkness can after Quang Tri Province. That cool crystal night when the moon sat plump and regal on a throne of clouds. When sparks crackled along the surface of my skin. When I could see with my third eye. When everything was desire—keen-edged and elastic. We all died that night and woke reformed. There was jasmine in the air. We all lifted our heads to catch the fragrance. Our eyes shut to better find the scent. We let it take us to our memories—winsome, fragile memories of love and coupling. I could see Camille—small, thin, gap-toothed girl—letting my unskilled lips and tongue taste her smooth dark skin. Seeing her, I reached for her. My hand held invisible fruit.

I have stories I can tell myself to mark the hours. I will know when it is morning. When it is light. Even if there are no sounds outside this darkness. I will know. I will feel the falsetto songs of the morning. I will feel men turning from sleep, reaching. I will know. I will feel them as they touch their tattooed places. I will feel them rub the memories they have pushed into their skin. I will feel the repetition of prayers, the flood of invectives, the proclamations of survival. I will know when it is morning and I will be fine.

I have learned from sitting with men in the dark. With the frightened, resigned, betrayed, and ecstatic. I have learned how to set myself flying. I have learned how to swim and to become water. I have learned how to billow.

No darkness can scare me. I have learned how to incandesce . . .

June 1, 1983

On October 2, 1982, my 26th birthday, David Lee proposed. Sort of. We were sitting in Rock Creek Park on the hill just down from the stables and the Nature Center. We both like the contour and feel of that hill. We used to go there a lot. Even though sometimes, it didn't smell very good. When I said something about the odor, he'd ask me what was I talking about. My farm boy. David says the hill is very female and reminds him of his mom. He said that every time we went. And every time he said it, he'd get this look. He'd squeeze his eyebrows and purse his lips. He does that to keep from crying. He doesn't think I know this. I remember all of a sudden he stood up, turned in a circle, and said, "Royce, you've got to marry me. Oh, shit." I was with him until the oh, shit part.

"We're already together. Why do I have to marry you? And why "Oh, shit?'" she said laughing.

"You have to marry me because . . . " He couldn't finish the sentence.

"Let's go home, David. I'm hungry. I want some cake," she said pulling grass.

"It's hard for me to put it into words," he said pacing.

"You're having trouble with words?" she asked, holding out her hand for him to help her up.

"Yes," he said sitting, "It's as if all the things I'm feeling are in a deep pond, full of water lilies. And I want to reach down and give you one of them but the roots are so complex. I just keep pulling and pulling and everything gets tangled. I can't say any more."

"Try." she said teasing.

"R.C. I've never let anyone know me the way you have. It's like you know how to pry me loose."

"Loose, from what?" she said reaching for his hand.

"From back burning," he said, surprising himself.

"Back burning?"

"Yeah. I have this way of clearing spaces by burning them away and you help me not to do that. Royce, I get myself into complicated situations because I'm not sure what kind of man I am."

"I hope you didn't practice this proposal," she said patting his leg and not hearing his seriousness.

"Royce, listen. Sometimes everything seems so pointless and I feel so powerless. I don't think I can change things. But you help me feel like maybe, maybe I can put myself to some use. You help me feel valuable and worthy. Can't you just marry me?"

"Sure," she said, pulling up blades of grass and putting them in David's lap.

"How soon?"

"How 'bout June? My mother would like that."

"Really? You really want to marry me?" he asked smiling broadly. "Yes. Why are you acting so peculiar? I love you. We live together, remember? Why would you think I wouldn't want to marry you?" she said holding his hand tightly.

"I don't know. How about next week or something."

"June, David. My mother only has one daughter. June."

June 2, 1983

He looked at me so sadly as if June were impossibly far away. What was it he knew? What didn't I hear? Why didn't I hear it?

Could I please have that day back?

As David says, rewind.

May 2, 1983

Dear Cammy,

Sorry to hear about David. Pop wrote me. I really like the brother. He and I used to have the deepest conversations after you had gone to bed. I can't say I agree with his politics, but he is definitely deep. Pop said things didn't go too well at the sentencing. He also said you didn't say anything for three weeks. I don't get why you took so long to tell them. It's not like you robbed the joint. Not that I'm glad or anything but it's just as well for me you're not tying the knot. I'm pretty sure my time won't be my own for a while. You know, you wouldn't have been truly married without Brother George as a witness. Speaking of weddings, I forgot the folks' anniversary. Could you please get me something for them? Get them something nice. They'll know you got it, but that's okay. They never seem to like my presents. I don't know why. The shit's always practical. I don't know why they didn't like the wheelbarrow. Anyway, I've enclosed an IOU for a hundred bucks. I'll send you the money as soon as the paymaster gets his act together. Got to go.

Brother George

June 5, 1983

With each
believing
the other
to be
a giver of love,
a sharer of sorrow,
a bringer of joy
and a reason for life,
Camille Royce Dumas
and
David Lesesne Carmichael
will be joined in holy union
on
Sunday, June 5, 1983
6:00 p.m.
at
All Souls
Unitarian Church
Washington, D.C.

Please join
Hunter Leon Dumas
and Ophelia David Royce Dumas
and
Michael Turblo Carmichael
in celebrating the union of their children.

When we first told Momma, she wanted me to wear Nana's dress. I told her I didn't think it would fit. She wanted us to have the reception at the Naval Club. She said with George in the Corps, somebody named Mrs. Ryans would help us. I told her we were going to have a celebration in Ft. Lincoln Park. Then she said, "It's your wedding." She looked so forlorn, I laughed at her. I told her it was our wedding but we wanted her to help us. Help, not control. Her little pout disappeared and she was back on Mrs. Ryans and Nana's dress.

I thought I would cry today. It's funny how you can plan sadness. I thought I would spend the day in bed thinking about David, thinking about me and David, and maybe doing some kind of ceremony. My Mom has called twice. How you doing, Sweetie? Doing all right?

I'm fine and part of me has no desire to dwell on what's not happening today. Another part wants to just wallow in it.

I think about David all the time. I've decided not to write until I find out what happened. I miss him. But I also don't. I'm not sure how I even have the gall to write that in this journal. It's not him that I don't miss. He'd flip over that sentence. It's the trouble I don't miss. I don't miss his angry letters. I don't miss feeling like I'm on 24-hour call. But I don't even know what that means. If none of this had happened and we had married, wouldn't I be on round-the-clock wife duty? That makes being a wife sound like being a security guard. I feel badly for not feeling worse. I know where he is is terrible. I'm afraid for him. I worry about his having been hurt . But I feel the walls. And I feel my fingernails are torn from trying to get over. And it hasn't even been 3 months. So what am I going to do for thirty years? What would I do if we had married? If we were marrying today? Will we ever talk about this? If nothing happens with his appeal, does he expect me to wait for thirty years? If nothing happens, what will I do without him? If nothing happens, what will I do with him? Now I get the oh, shit part.

. . . No, you may not

Mama, may I take 12 giant steps

No, you may not

Mama, may I take 11 umbrella steps

No, you may not

Mama, may I take 10 elephant steps

No, you may not

Mama, may I take 9 banana split steps

No, you may not

Mama, may I take 8 gorilla steps

No, you may not

Mama, may I take 7 camel steps

No, you may not

Mama, may I take 6 lion steps

No, you may not

Mama, may I take 5 ostrich steps

No, you may not

Mama, may I take 4 rabbit steps

No, you may not

Mama, may I take 3 turtle steps

No, you may not

Mama, may I take 2 baby steps

No, you may not

Mama, may I take 1 snail step . . .

David! David! Stop playing with me like that! Nobody's telling you no. Nobody except the nobody in your head. Don't be trifling with yourself. Don't be trifling with me either. Who's Mama, if it ain't me? And I've never told you no. In fact, Mr. David Lesesne Carmichael, I'm the one who's been telling you to take steps. Now if this playing with yourself is just something you got to do 'cause you in the hole, think again. You ain't never been out as far as I can see. You got to make a life before you can make a new one. And you got to make a life before it can be taken away. Hmm, Mama, may I. Ain't that some stuff. If you got to do it, you better try Daddy, may I. Lord, these children wear me out.

June 10, 1983

I hope that last entry was grief. I hope all that stuff will go back into the boxes it came out of. I've decided I should probably keep writing to him, even if I don't send the letters. That way, he'll stay real to me. What does that mean, stay real to me? How could he be any more real.

More and more it seems like I'm David, like I have no life as Camille. That's not David's fault. That's mine. Maybe it's not my fault either. Point is, I need to concentrate more on myself. I can't do anything for David while he's in isolation. Maybe I can do something for myself while he's in, while we're both in. We're not both in. I just mean . . . I don't know what I mean.

Green light . . .

Red Light.

No! You got to go back.

Green light . . .

Red light.

Green light . . .

Is that better, Mama?

Since you so busy telling me everything, tell me how to get the hell out of here. Or don't your powers extend that far? Seems to me, you had your own troubles escaping and that you played a few games yourself.

Red Light.

Thought you were going to get me.

Go on back.

Green Light . . .

As far as that playing games stuff is concerned, it takes one to know one, David Lee. It takes one to know one.

June 15, 1983

I had another dream about David's mother. She was tall and slender. Her gaze was direct. Her eyes were beautiful but I can't remember the color. She could've spit David out. She had this long, thick braid. She seemed just a little older than me. David says she was 39 when she died. She had on a yellow dress and looked quite seductive. I was sitting on the porch of a home I don't ever remember visiting. Mrs. Carmichael walked up the steps carrying a basket of yams and squash. She kissed me on the cheek and handed me a fan. "You're gonna need a fan, " she said. I thanked her and offered her a chair. We drank lemonade together and then went for a swim in this river that seemed to be right in back of the house. I remember that we were naked and I was struck by how lovely she was and I wondered if she thought I was lovely and if I would be a good wife for David. Then she was gone. Next thing, I heard rattlesnake sounds. But I knew it was just Mrs. Carmichael and I didn't need to be afraid.

. . . I lie down

I am born every day

I am the dweller in the limits of the earth

I renew myself

I become young every day

May my heart be to me in the House of Hearts

I lie down

I am born every day

I am the dweller in the limits of the earth

I renew myself

I become young every day

May my heart be light

How can my heart be light

When I have been so good at killing?

Camille? Ooooh, Honey. Don't it get hot. You'd think with all the trees around here, it'd be cool. You got any more of that lemonade? David's all right. He can forget how strong he is. I got to remind him from time to time. He don't like the dark. Sometimes, he and Catherine had to run out into the fields at night. He always had him a flashlight. "And the light shineth in darkness; and the darkness comprehended it not." That's St. John, don't you know.

Don't worry. I'm looking after him.

We'll help each other, you and I. There wasn't nobody to help me. I wished I coulda run away. Don't know why I didn't 'cept I was scared. The only thing is I was scared anyway.

Sure could use some more of that lemonade.

June 19, 1983

I went to visit Baderinwa at the hospital yesterday. She has a little boy, Nathaniel Dunbar Hendricks. Born at 8:09 yesterday morning. He weighs 7 lbs. 7 oz. and is 19 inches long. I came as she was nursing Nathaniel. Baderinwa reminded me it was Father's Day. She asked me if I would get her a card for Robert. I didn't want to but I did. I went over to the Safeway. I got three. One for her and two for me. For the New Father, For My Husband, and From Your Daughter With Love. We had just finished signing them when Robert came in. He was so proud. He was about to burst. He put his arm around Baderinwa and squeezed her shoulder. I didn't stay long after that. I went to the bathroom and threw up. I hated how they looked together. So happy. I hated how they kept looking at each other like theirs was the only baby in the world. They acted like they were going to get a certificate of achievement because they had made a baby. They'll find out, Nathaniel's just on loan.

I stopped by Taylor Street to see Daddy.

Do you think about Father's Day, David? Do you even have an idea what day it is?

This has been a difficult day.

June 20, 1983

Work was good today. The other material finally came from some of the branches. Buchi Emecheta. Delia Dominguez, Lynne Alvarez, Mary Crow, Bessie Head, Efua Sutherland, Ama Ata Aidoo, Claribel Alegria, Ulalume Gonzalez de Leon. I love their names. Not all of them are poets. But that's all right. I'll switch things around.

David, what do you think of "In the Garden Where I Write" as a title for my display? It's from a poem by de Leon. I like it. I like it a lot.

I can't wait to put everything together. If we ever have a little girl, I'm going to name her Ulalume. Ulalume Carmichael. Maybe not.

June 21, 1983

The first day of Summer. I went up to the park and watched the sun set in the west and the moon rise in the east. It was wonderful. The colors were like the insides of tropical fruits and melons. Then came the ocean blushes and eggplant hues . It made me want to go to the islands. David said he would take me. I wanted to sit under a tree and eat flying fish, plantain, doved peas, and coconut pie. Someone was singing and playing the guitar over in the playground. All I needed was the ocean.

I came home and said my prayers. They weren't very good. My heart's too confused. I asked if I could just look at the sunset or the moon without feeling guilty. I asked if I could be my own little island, just for a while.

Daddy says he doesn't go to church because you have to be careful what you pray for. Amen.

June 22, 1983

Momma came over this evening and took me to dinner. She asked me what I had a taste for and I said Caribbean food. We compromised on seafood. We went down to The Flagship and stuffed ourselves with rum buns and red snapper. The waiter flirted with Momma and she liked it. "Don't tell your father," she said. She doesn't want me to tell so she can tell him herself. She wants to make sure he knows she's with him because she wants to be, not because she doesn't have any other choices.

That would be nice.

June 23, 1983

Today was my long day at the library. This morning, I signed up for a workshop on computer systems and public information. The workshop was full by lunch time. Supposedly, the workshop facilitator is very good looking. The new girl from the Woodbridge branch told me I should take my name off the list to give the single girls a chance. She was serious.

June 24, 1983

Maybe I could organize The 1983 Grass Widows Convention. Barbados would be good. I wonder how many would come? How much should our dues be?

June 25, 1983

Dear David and Camille,

Who are you? I want to get to know you. Do you want to know me?

Camille Royce

Camille

Royce

R.C.

Cammy

me

July 2, 1983

I can't say a lot for 26. The only good thing is that I didn't lose my mother. I came very close. That should have taught me something.

I want to talk to her. I want to sit with her in her sewing room and tell her how I am turned inside out. I can't do this now. For some reason, she's worried about George. George is her normal child. My brother likes things simple. High school. Marines. He's not really a patriot. He believes in the mechanics of the service. George says he loves the Marine Corps because everything is straightforward. You meet some guys. You work with them. You go places. You do your job. Everyone stays healthy. You go more places. Simple.

Is it simple, George?

I envy you, Road Runner.

July 9, 1983

I haven't done well at writing David. Actually, I haven't written him at all. I have been working extra hours at the library. Filling in. I've been thinking about a part-time job. I could use the money. I could use the time away from the apartment.

I have killed almost all the plants since David has been gone. Not intentionally. I'm just not good with plants like he is. I have been thinking about boxing up his stuff. I need to take his clothes out of the closet. I already put his toiletries under the sink. I feel like this is some sort of betrayal, but am I supposed to look at his stuff forever?

I can be so melodramatic. Three and a half months is not forever.

I talked to Nichols yesterday. He says he calls the prison every couple of weeks to see how David is doing and so they know someone is watching. We owe him a lot of money. He doesn't seem to be concerned. He likes David very much. They were in Viet Nam at the same time. Nichols is about seven years older than David. He says he misses his conversations with him. He says he is working hard to get him out. David's father and his brother never answered my letter. They never sent any addresses. Nichols says that's just as well. Unless David knew a Supreme Court justice or Charlton Heston, it probably wouldn't help. We both laughed about David Lee and Charlton Heston being friends. Nichols is kind. He asked me how I was doing. He told me he'd let me know as soon as he heard something about the appeal.

George's birthday is next week. Momma says she's gonna send that wheelbarrow to him. and see how he likes it.

Baderinwa called me last night to say she was coming back to the library the first week in August. She also called to coo about her baby. This is my best friend. I guess it doesn't occur to her that I don't want to hear about Nathaniel. It's not really her fault. There's a lot she doesn't know.

Daddy wants me to join his bowling league. He also says there's a lot of good-looking men in his league. Daddy has never been subtle.

Spence, it's funny don't you think. You saving my life in Nam. Me not saving your life here. Me doing life for us both. I've been laughing. Have you?

I want to fuck. Someone grown I can carry in one arm. Someone who will hold on to my neck loosely. Someone whose whisper will singe the folds of my ear. Someone who knows every lie I've ever wanted to hear. Someone who will let me go. Someone I can slide under the door. Someone who will let me out. Someone who will not follow me home.

Spence? Who's Spence? And why does he keep laughing?

Oh, yeah, Spence. Comrade in arms. I guess it is funny, brother.

Why the hell did you mark me?

Maybe when a grenade has to detonate, a grenade has to detonate.

Is that right, motherfucker? You the one all up into Camus and shit. What's the existential spin on our predicament?

Let's say today is October 2, 1982. It's Royce's birthday. But I don't ask her to marry me. And I don't tell her my doubts about myself. And I don't make love to her like it's a qualifying heat. And I don't feel like I have always loved her. And we don't make a baby. And I leave her that night. Would I still end up here?

Let's say it's April 22, 1971. And it's my Mom's birthday. And I'm 17. But I don't try to stick-up Moon's Liquor Store with a toy gun. And I never see Delahaney. And I never have a lawyer who makes great deals and talks me out of a record. And my father speaks to me again. And my brother acts like he knows me. And I don't enlist in the service. What then?

Let's say it's November 22, 1982 but I don't go home. And I don't recognize Spence on Stuart Street. And we don't go for a drink. And he doesn't start talking about all his failures. And I don't start thinking about mine. And he doesn't have a gun. And we don't drive by the So-Lo Station. And the cashier stays cool. And Spence doesn't go crazy. And I don't sit in the car thinking, "What the fuck am I doing?" And I don't let one of the customers get away and call the cops. And the cashier doesn't get shot. And the cops don't come. And Spence doesn't die. And they don't find me daydreaming in Spence's Pontiac. And they don't pull me from the car. And I don't see Spence. And I don't call, "Medic." And I don't see the ambulance. And I don't have the shit kicked out of me. And I never have to call Royce or Daddy. Would I be ripping up my clothes, tying pieces around my fingers to remember what day it is in the dark?

Yeah, Spence. I just need to keep my ass home on anniversaries.

Isn't every day an anniversary, Spence? Oh, I get it. No wonder you're laughing.

July 17, 1983

I've been making an island, David.

You're everywhere. All around me for miles and miles just like the ocean.

How can I make a bridge when there is no place to reach?

July 18, 1983

David!

You're in the stacks at the library. You're the old man who takes a book from the shelf, holds it close to his face, flips the pages, places the book back on the shelf, and begins again.

You're the thin, young men who want materials on Malcolm.

You're the children who gather their little chairs in a circle for Saturday morning storytelling.

How is it you're all these people? I can't look up anything without finding some reference to you.

July 24, 1983

Dear David and Camille,

You need a vacation from distance, secrets, indifference, time, crimes, and miscarriages.

Where can you go?

Where can we go?

Where can I go?

Damn. Who wrote that? Me or David?

July 25, 1983

Dear David and Camille,

I went over to Momma and Daddy's last night. Daddy was watching Sarah Vaughan on the television. I was standing in the hallway watching him watch her. She was singing a slow tune, one I hadn't heard before. He patted his slippered feet together, rocked his head, and held on to the chair. I don't know if it was the words or the way she was singing or just Sarah, but the song cracked me open and pulled the last nine months from me. There in the hallway, with Sarah singing, "Once in A While," I burst into tears. Daddy was crying, too.

Ophelia took Camille into the bedroom. They sat on the bed together. As Camille cried, she plucked the little, fuzzy white balls on the bed spread. Ophelia brushed her fingers away. "We've had this spread for 22 years and you still got to try and tear it up." Her daughter did not laugh or raise her head. Ophelia reached for the box of tissue on her night stand and placed it between them.

Camille tried to speak. She wanted to tell her mother everything—the baby, David's family, her inability to decide what she should do next.

"What now, Camille? I can't understand, Baby. Tell Momma, again." Camille was crying so hard, Ophelia got up and took the towel from the bathroom doorknob. She put it in her daughter's hands. She held Camille's shoulders and said, "Wet it up good, Baby. Let go all your hurt. Cry yourself a river."

Camille was surprised by how much grief and fluid she contained. She gave herself a headache crying. She made herself limp and slit-eyed. She could not remember what she had said and what she had withheld. As her tears finally subsided, she became aware of her father standing in the doorway watching her whimper. Camille saw on her father's face, the same expression that David carried the afternoon he struggled with his marriage proposal. Ophelia covered her daughter's shoulders with one of her afghans and left the room.

"Camille, why did you wait so long to tell?" Hunter asked. She hadn't been aware of his listening. Now that she was empty, she could barely hear. Her father's strong tobacco scent reached her like a memory. It made Camille feel safe.

"Daddy, just now, when you were looking at me, what were you thinking?"

"I was thinking about the Dismal," he said stroking her head.

"What?"

"The Great Dismal near home."

"I don't understand. What are you talking about?"

"Well . . . remember when you were about 12, your brother was 15 and we went to Suffolk for the family reunion."

"Yes, Daddy. That's when I first met David."

"Um-um. You see, the Dumas side of the family was in Southampton County and the Perrys—David's Mama's family—was over there in Henry County. Now, your great grandfather Hunter Dumas married Lorraine Perry. Lorraine Perry was the sister of Joshua, Cora Lee, Melroy, Edith, and somebody whose name I forget. Joshua married Clotilde Scott. They had Lesesne and some other children. Then Lesesne married Ardelia Winters and they had a bunch a children one of whom was David's Mama Janeece."

"Daddy, my head hurts and you're confusing me. What do David's people have to do with the Dismal? What is the Dismal?"

"I was just going over some territory so you'd . . . you'd get the big picture."

"Please, Daddy."

"Well now, the folks that come out Southampton County were not your average Colored people. They tended to be the children of folks who tried every way they could to escape."

"So average Colored people don't try..."

"Yeah, alright. What I was trying to say was . . ."

"You're going way back now, right?"

"Well, yes and no. If you'd just give me a chance to get a whole sentence out, maybe I could explain."

"Sorry, Daddy but I don't know if I want to go back into all that."

"Well, we're not talking about what you want right this minute. As I was saying...people been trying to escape all kinds of things, all kinds of ways, from way back times to right this minute. Only thing is we don't generally note that all the things are really just one thing. You know what I'm saying?

"Now. Some of the people that was running away long time ago, ran to the Dismal. Fact is, some folks believe there are still people living in that swamp today. The Dismal was and is a treacherous place. Poisonous everything. Flowers. Vipers. Insects. Probably even had poisonous birds. Now. Used to be the White folks tried to drain that sucker. They used all number of men, most of them slaves, to try and bleed the life out of the Dismal. The canals would fill up then they'd drain right back into the swamp. That's right."

She looked over at the clock on his bureau wondering how long it would be before her father got to his main point.

"Hold on, I'm getting there," he said patting her hand. "Because it was so treacherous, it was awful hard for dogs to track the runaways. And, it was hard for horses to get around in there to gather people up. But you know White folks are not easily deterred. Specially them hard ass motherfuckers, excuse my French, who took somebody running away as a personal insult. They rode their horses in there and rode some of those folks to death. So, some of the runaways got captured and got sent back to the plantations they came from and most times they were made into examples. But the way I heard it, most folks didn't get captured."

"What happened, Daddy?"

"Well, some folks died. Some folks got turned around and ended up headed back to the Big House. Some folks went back to the plantation after they felt the barbs the Dismal had to offer. They went back under their own steam. But some other folks just stayed in the swamp and tried to make do. Met people from all over the region in there. 'Cause you know they came to the Dismal from North Carolina, too. They had their families in there. Hunted in there. Did the best they could do in there. In the swamp, wasn't freedom but wasn't slavery neither. Thing was they were so close and yet so far."

"What do you mean?"

"Well, the Dismal's not more than 20 miles from the ocean. You know there were probably days the runaways could smell the salt of the sea. That had to make them hungry. Almost being home."

Ophelia came back in with a tray. She had made tea in her good china pot and had poured some into her special Sunday cups; the ones with saucers. It was Ophelia's way of simultaneously marking their time together as important and chastising Camille for behaving like a stranger. She had a talent for feeding two birds with one hand. She had cut a piece of pie for Hunter. He didn't care for tea, said it was too dainty.

"Why did my crying make you think of all that."

"Wasn't your crying," he said as he moved a bite of a pie around his mouth, "was your grief. Your great grandfather used to tell me about all the folks from the Dumas plantation that eased themselves over to Dismal. Camille, he'd tell these stories that scared me as a boy. I used to check the ground out with a stick, worried about being swallowed up by the ground like the Dismal swallowed so many who came seeking refuge. At the same time, the stories made me feel kind of glad. Proud. He told this one about a man—a strong worker, the kind they prize—who ran away time after time and who was found dead, hanging from a cypress tree with his chain and harness dangling from him."

"Hunter, why would you tell the child that one?" Ophelia asked.

"She's got to understand that sometimes all you can do is choose how you gonna die. That's all the freedom you gonna get."

"I still don't see why that lesson's so necessary tonight."

"You know they say Nat Turner hid out in the Dismal when he was first thinking on his rebellion. A little like Christ in the wilderness, don't you think?" Hunter said, changing the subject. The three sat silently as they thought and tried not to think about life in the Dismal. Camille and Ophelia drank their tea. Hunter ate his pie.

"That look you had on your face was just like David's the day he asked me to marry him," Camille said after their moments of silence.

"What did you say to the boy?"

"He was acting so peculiar that day. David is usually so certain about everything and everybody."

"That's the truth," Ophelia added.

"But that day, he was acting . . ."

"Scared?"

"Yeah. I guess . . . Agitated. That's more like it."

"Like I said, what did you say?"

"I asked him why was he acting so strange."

"Man asks you to marry him and you tell him he was acting strange?" Hunter asked.

"Yes, what's wrong with that? It was my birthday not Valentine's Day. I wasn't thinking about getting married. He just caught me off balance."

"Talk to your daughter, Ophelia," Hunter said as he left the room.

"What's wrong? I don't get it?" Camille said, placing her cup on the tray and pulling the afghan around her.

"Camille, your father is a big man," Ophelia said pouring herself more tea. "On the day he asked me to marry him, you would have thought he was four feet tall. He was pacing, fidgety, pulling on his clothes, tugging at his collar. The man was pitiful. He had taken a bath in cologne. You know, he was on the trucks then and he was always worried about smelling like garbage to me. And I didn't understand him just like you didn't understand David. But I had enough sense to be quiet and listen. Finally, he said, "Girl, we don't have a chance in the world. Marry me."

"That's almost exactly what David said."

"As far as I can tell, your Daddy and maybe David, looked out on the world and felt small. Now, I know your daddy loved me when he asked me to marry him. But he was also afraid and lonely and hoping maybe together we'd be all right. And I think he thought having a wife would make him try all the harder at the same time that he was scared to death of failing in front of me. Your daddy came up very hard, as I believe David did, and a lot of times he gets by on bravado. He doesn't believe he can do something until it's almost done. This is at the same time that he knows there's not a stronger, better man in the world. That's the tricky part. The way your father talks, you'd think he was fearless. But he's afraid. I want you to understand. There's not a cowardly bone in your father's body but he has lived with fear and doubt all his life. For the longest time, your Daddy couldn't figure out how it was that the world was run by people weaker and not nearly as good as he was. It would keep him up at night."

"And now, Momma?"

"And now there are days when he knows he can move the world a couple of inches to the left and days when getting up is all he can do. I'd say your father's life is one foot in front of the other."

"What do you mean? He doesn't plan? What?"

"No, Honey. Your daddy is the original planner. He's always turning something around, mulling it over, taking it into careful consideration. He prides himself on his thoughtfulness. That's not the point."

"What do you mean then?"

"Your daddy knows that he can devise the most astute, comprehensive plan that's ever been made and sometimes it's not going to be enough."

"And so . . ."

"And so, he plans each day knowing something may happen that will turn the world upside down."

"David says that."

"Um-um. I'm sure he does. You want to stay over?"

"Yes, please."

"I think there's linen on your bed."

"Mommy, how long did it take you to figure out Daddy?"

"I'm still working on it. You can't ever think you really know somebody. If you do, you probably about to take him for granted. The trick is sometimes you got to keep your mouth shut and your ears open. And you got to do that without resentment. It doesn't matter if it seems like you're the one who always has a shut mouth. It hurts and it's unfair and it makes you angry and you feel like you could slap somebody. But it doesn't matter because it's necessary. And you got to learn how to watch them fall, and not fall with them. And you got to make them believe all you saw falling was their shadow. I don't know how it is to be married to a white man. Could be the same thing but I doubt it seriously. And I don't know how it is for a woman who decides to forget the whole thing and be with another woman. But if you are going to be married to a Black man . . . Hon-ey."

"Mommy? What do you think is going to happen to David?"

"Baby, I wish I knew."

"What should I do?"

"Do what you're doing as long as you can and then do something else."

"That's it. That's the great advice I've been waiting for?"

"All I can tell you is what I do myself. Take this tray in for me, would you?"

"Night."

"Good night, Baby."

Camille took the tray into the kitchen, washed the dishes, cut the lights out, and sat in the darkness. Her father came around to check the windows and doors and to kiss her goodnight.

July 26, 1983

One more month, David. One more month. One more. Anything can happen in a month.

These folks been testifyin as long as I've been livin. Testifyin longer. All them words. Enough to float you a battleship. All I want to know is, you any closer to understanding?

175. The Blackstone Family - 5 members

176. The Middleton Family - 15 members

177. The Fairfax Family - 22 members

178. The Maddox Family - 102 members

179. The Grayson Family - 2 members

180. The Hayes Family - 13 members

181. The Jamison Family - 29 members

182. The Evans Family - 43 members

183. Martin Graham , a freed black

184. Mister General, a freed black

185. The Lineless Family - 7 members

186. The Pipsco Family - 2 members

187. The Pinkney Family - 205 members

188. The Coombes Family - 2 members

189. Oliver Hampton, a free man of color

189. Nolinda Mitchell, a freed black

191. Phenix Henderson, a freed black

192. The Widdecomb Family - 181 members

193. The Robeson Family - 4 members

194. The McGrundy Family - 31 members

195. Worthy Dangerfield, a freed black

196. Rachel Armisted, a free woman of color

197. Wheel Clement, a free man of color

198. Mary Syphax, a freed black

199. Proctor Lowe, a freed black

200. Acquila Pearson, a freed black

201. The Cephas Family - 5 members

202. The Hollyday Family - 2 members

203. Gladden Rideout and Guardian, freed blacks

204. Verlinda, a slave

205. Magruder Gates, a freed black

206. Toyer Burrell, a free person of color

207. Careful Jefferson, a free person of color

208. Coffie DeShield, a free person of color

209. Thankful Dickinson, a freed black

210. Sarah Swanson, a freed black

211. Constance Wharton, a free woman of color

. . . I lie down
I am born every day . . .

You who have stared down these walls and this little space, whisper to me how it is done. I am afraid. They will not tell me how many days I have been here. My calendar has failed me. My hands are numb from trying to mark the days. I have no more stories left and I am afraid. Please?

There is a place, beyond my father's house that is tranquil.

There is a place, beyond my father's house where sunlight filters through the trees and makes a church.

There is a place, beyond my father's house where he doesn't beat us.

There is a place, beyond my father's house where I pray.

There is a place, beyond my father's house where my mother dances.

There is a place, beyond my father's house that yields to me.

There is a place, beyond my father's house where I have stashed my memories.

There is a place, beyond my father's house where I know they are safe.

There is a place, beyond my father's house where I can see.

There is a place, beyond my father's house where there's a future.

There is a place, beyond my father's house where my son watches butterflies.

There is a place, beyond my father's house where all is peace.

There is a place, beyond my father's house where jasmine grows.

There is a place, beyond my father's house where I eat apples.

There is a place, beyond my father's house where we make love.

There is a place, beyond my father's house where I read Baldwin.

There is a place, beyond my father's house where my wife can rest.

There is a place, beyond my father's house where there is

laughter.

There is a place, beyond my father's house where there are swings.

There is a place, beyond my father's house where there is fresh water.

There is a place, beyond my father's house where time goes by.

There is a place, beyond my father's house where my daughter sings.

There is a place, beyond my father's house where we are people.

There is a place, beyond my father's house where we are free.
There is a place, beyond my father's house where I am heroic.

There is a place, beyond my father's house where I will die.

Thank you.

August 5, 1983
8:16 p.m.

Dearest David,

It was 102° today. The paper said it was not quite so hot in Richmond but I am sure it is stifling where you are. I wish this letter were a cool breeze and sweet water.

Thank you for my journal. It has helped me. I love you for it. I love you (period).

I have written you many letters that I will not send you. They are too much. I talked to Mr. Nichols yesterday and asked him to make sure that I can see you Labor Day Weekend.

I have been saving magazines for you. Should I bring them or mail them to you? I asked Daddy why you would need these magazines. I think you must be growing on him. He said, "the man's going to arm himself with words." He said it like he understands you. I asked him if he meant literally or figuratively and he said, "Ophelia, come talk to your daughter."

I am convinced there is a way for us to be together through this. It requires me to shift my expectations of you. *Not lessen them. Shift them.* It requires me to ask more of myself. I have to find the balance between recognizing where we are and resisting it.

Camille

August 5, 1983

I went to Baderinwa's today. She lives in Takoma Park now. Her grandmother left her a house. She's lucky. The house is surrounded by trees and it was nice and cool there. We talked for a little while. Mostly she talked. She asked me about the library and told me she wasn't coming back after all. Robert told her that with the house being paid for and with him putting aside a little extra, she could stay home for a year if she wanted to. This seemed to make her very happy. Robert has never seemed that kind. It felt like a cozy little trap to me. He used to always complain about the men who would flirt with her at the check-out and renewal counter. I could be wrong. Maybe he really cares about her and Nathaniel and he's trying his best to make this work. Besides, if Baderinwa is happy, who am I to judge? It's probably just an acute case of jealousy.

I asked her if I could hold Nathaniel. It was very painful. I sat with him in their rocking chair and let him play with my earring. It was good but it was painful.

I'm going to let my letters to David say the easy things. The complicated things should be said face to face or here. I want to plan on visiting him once a month. A routine will help both of us.

I haven't been feeling well lately. I should have gone back to the doctor in May. I didn't feel like having to talk about the miscarriage. Momma's been really helpful. She had a miscarriage before I was born. I didn't know that until last week. Momma went seven months. That was probably a lot worse than five. She said that she and Daddy could hardly speak to each other.

"It wasn't because he blamed me or I felt guilty. We were both just too damned sad." Camille had never heard her mother cuss. "We tried again right away and we were very glad to see your silly face."

"What do I do, Momma? Us trying again is a little difficult," Camille asked angrily.

"I guess you've got to try again in other ways. I don't know, Baby," Ophelia said calmly, "Why don't you find yourself a nice woman doctor and get some advice?"

"What about Dr. Andrews?"

"I've been going to Dr. Andrews for a hundred years but he's not the most sensitive man. He's a good doctor but no confidante. Your feeling poorly may have more to do with leavings than illness. Babies like to leave something of themselves behind," Ophelia said, reaching for her daughter's hand.

"I know."

July 4, 1983

Hey, Cammy!

Just a quick note to say I love you all very much. Everything is fine.

You know, Consuela still writes me. Her letters set the mailbags on fire, you hear me. I've been charging $2.50 to read them. I've made over $600.00 bucks in IOUs. It's lousy of me, I know. But at least I know I'm a dog. Don't tell her I'm pimping her letters. If you see her, tell her I miss her. I really do. I'll be glad when we get out of this holding pattern. We need to just go ahead and do whatever damage we're going to do.

How are you doing? How's the library? Maybe you should go back to school and get your library degree. All right. I'll stay out of your business.

Like I said, just a quick one. Take care of yourself. Give everyone a big hug. Is Pop still smoking? Make him stop, will you?

Love,
George

Camille? How come you don't call on me? I'm the only one knows how David's doing. Seems to me, you'd ask. I'll tell you anyway. He's getting a little thin, but his hard head is keeping him in the game. He's a little scared of how it's going to be when he gets out of isolation. Keep writing him, Sweetheart. Keep writing. Even if you can't make sense out of it. Keep on.

August 19, 1983

I shouldn't have to apologize to David for losing the baby but I will. Maybe it will make some space for us to breathe. Maybe it's old news he'd rather not hear again.

I keep thinking that talking to him about it is a good idea, a bad idea, a good idea, a bad idea. Kind of like He Loves Me, He Loves Me Not.

August 19, 1983
7:35 a.m.

Dearest David,

I went to the doctor on Wednesday. Momma had suggested it. I wasn't feeling good and I had never followed-up the miscarriage properly. I decided not to go back to Dr. Andrews. Baderinwa got me an appointment with her doctor, Jennifer Majors. Dr. Majors is about ten years older than me and we hit it off well. She's really great! I felt like I was going to an older sister for help.

She took a lot of time with me. She was so easy to talk to. Easier than Momma or Baderinwa. I didn't feel like I had to prove anything or hold something back. I told her how much I wanted the baby and how much I loved you and how I had all these grand plans for telling everyone at Thanksgiving. I told her how everything seemed to go wrong and that I felt if only I had told you before you went home, you never would have gone. I told her about Momma miscarrying. I told her how guilty I have felt for not telling you in time and how badly I feel for losing the baby. She was kind to me, David, and I needed her kindness.

You've never asked me much about what happened and I haven't been forthcoming with details. I've felt your disappointment in me. I couldn't figure out what to say that would lessen that.

It may be way too late, David, for me to say I'm sorry. But I am really sorry. I'm sorry I didn't catch you on the way out the door and make you stay. I'm sorry that the baby's gone. Please forgive me.

Camille

August 20, 1983
6:00 p.m.

Beloved,

Hopefully, by the time I get to Richmond on September 4, you will have read my letters. We have all been praying that you are well.

With all my love,
Camille

August 20, 1983

I could stop writing.

wednesday, august 31, 1983
camille,

i am very tired. i have read your letters. reading them was difficult. i want to see you. i am not angry with you.

your husband,

david

thursday, september 1, 1983

camille,

i have been around the world. i have been outside of myself.

i have been in the dark so long, the light is daunting. i have to take things slowly. i was moved to another cell.

most of my things were taken. a muslim brother has lent me this paper. he has lent me a pen. he has given me four stamps. he will mail this for me. allahu-akbar.

your husband

friday, september 2, 1983

mr. and mrs. dumas,

i love camille very much. please make her go away.

allahu-akbar.

david lesesne carmichael

saturday, september 3, 1983

camille,

please bring me soap. please bring me 7 lemons. please bring me a toothbrush. please bring me a book. please bring me a photograph. please bring some honeysuckle. please hurry. allahu-akbar.

your husband

September 5, 1983
2:55 a.m.

Dear David,

It's 226 miles round trip from our apartment to Spring Street. I drove down to see you as I said I would. They wouldn't let me in. My clothing was illegal. I was illegal. A felony—inciting to riot. I had on a pair of jeans, a leotard, a long-sleeved, buttoned-up work shirt, headwrap, socks, and sneakers. I expected them to make me undo my wrap. They did. A guard took the cloth and shook it out. She let it drag on the floor. I'm surprised she didn't step on it. Feeling my breasts in the pat down, the guard told me I wouldn't be allowed in because I didn't have legal underwear. She called in another guard who also patted me down to determine if my breasts were too provocative. Officer Clemons said I definitely needed a holster for my weapons. They called in two more male guards to discuss the matter at length. The four decided that my breasts were too arousing and that I shouldn't be let in. By the time the Breast Committee finished its deliberations, there was only an hour left of visiting time. I argued that nothing showed and that I had intentionally covered my body as much as possible. The major on shift suggested I go to a department store and buy a brassiere. He would allow me to change in the facility and still see you. That was *if* I could get back in a half hour. They didn't let anyone in during the last 30 minutes. I asked if there was some way I could let you know I was there. Commander Duffy stated that it was too much trouble for his men to call you off of the block just to give you a message. So, I left. Please understand.

Royce

P.S. You should be receiving office supplies and stamps very soon. My parents are sending you a care package. Please, please understand.

Yes. I will wait.
I will wait as long as I must.
I will wait as long as I can.
What else can I do?

Dear Friend,
When you get this letter, kiss someone you love and make magic. This letter has been sent to you for good luck. It has been around the world nineteen times. You will receive good luck within four days of receiving this letter providing you send it back out. Send copies to people you think need good luck. Don't send money as fate has no price. Do not keep this letter. It must leave your hands within 96 hours. Since the letter must make a tour of the world, you must make 20 copies and send them to your friends and associates. After a few days, you will get a surprise. This is true even if you are not superstitious. Please send no money. Please don't ignore this. It works.

Your Friend

September 5, 1983
Dear David,

Before you say anything, I am not calling the warden. I am not filing a complaint. I am going to leave it alone. I am not going back until Daddy can go with me.

September 6, 1983
Dear David,

Somebody sent me a chain letter. I don't know who. It was unsigned. I should have responded long ago but I can't think of 20 people I really dislike enough to send it to. I thought about sending it to some of the wild boys down there with you but I couldn't digest the irony.

Royce—

How could you not come?

How could you not come?

How could you not come?

How could you not come?

How could you not come?

Baby, tell me, please.

Thursday, September 14, 1983
9:25 p.m.

Baby—

i got your letter. i have to tell you, your absence was worse than isolation. i needed to see you. i really needed to see you. But i do understand. It's taken me a little while to get over my disappointment. You need to talk to Nichols about filing a formal complaint. my appeal is being heard in three weeks. Right in time for your birthday. i know that you appreciate how difficult it is in here for me. But it is especially difficult when i anticipate your arrival and then am robbed of the time i have looked forward to so ardently. You might consider other options. You might talk to Cedrick. He wrote and said he plans to see me for my birthday. i would much prefer that you come with my brother than by yourself. i hesitate to ask, but when are you planning to come back? Baby, please come soon. Next time, if you have a problem, stay overnight, call Nichols, and try to see me again the next day. Don't give up so quickly.

Yours,
David

He promised himself that he would not take things out on her that didn't belong to her. For the life of him, an absurd expression for him to use, he couldn't understand why she would tell him the details of her attempts to see him. Doesn't she get it? Why can't she get it? If he can't do anything about it, he'd just as soon she'd keep it to herself. He is not willing to go into segregation again. Not for anyone. Not for any thing. Not ever again.

September 21, 1983
10:05 p.m.

Dear David,

You're right, I should have stayed over in Richmond and tried to see you the next day. But I couldn't think of that at the time. I wanted to see you, too. I felt dirty and needed to come home to get clean.

The drive home was difficult. I probably shouldn't have been driving at all. I kept replaying the scenes in the prison over and over and then I'd look up from somewhere in those reruns and find myself miles later down the road, not remembering other cars, the scenery, not even the sounds from the cassette player beside me in the passenger seat. Mostly, I thought about the walk from the parking lot to the front gate. VCF is such a strange facility. It sits there in the middle of the city like some kind of high rise. The men at the windows called me whatever names their memories and penises demanded. I pretended that you were one of them, watching me. Is that sick? I wondered what that would mean to you, seeing me, hearing them, knowing all the reasons on their side, knowing me. Did you hear them? I don't know how the hell I got home.

I was going through my album last night. One of my favorite photographs is you and George at the reunion at Uncle Leonard's house. I think he may have been the only one in the family who was not afraid of you and I being together. There's another photograph of him alone leaning towards a birthday cake blowing out candles. He's smiling and painted with candlelight. He's making a wish.

I had a dream about the two of you the other night. I was watching him through binoculars. He was trying to cross a mine field. He had a stick that he tapped gently on the ground. He stepped lightly along the path of the stick.

Then you came along. You were running from the other end of the field with your arms flailing about. To him, it looked like you were laughing, saying come on, hurry up, stop being so goddamned careful. But through the binoculars, I could see you were warning him to go back. You called his name. Just as he looked up, he misstepped. I woke up.

I haven't dreamed about your mother in a long time. I wonder if she's disappointed in me, too.

I'm going to try and get there for your birthday. I spoke to my Dad. He said he'd let me know tomorrow. David, I can't come with Cedrick. I just can't.

Love,
Royce

P.S. I really miss your poems! Could you send me one please?

Tuesday, September 27, 1983
7:00 a.m.

Royce—

i promised myself that i would not take things out on you that don't belong to you. For the life of me, an absurd expression for me to use, i can't understand why you would tell me the details of your attempts to see me. Don't you get it? Why can't you get it? If i can't do anything about something, i'd just as soon you'd keep it to yourself. i am not willing to go into segregation again. For anyone. For anything. Ever. i know you're not coming today. i know you're not coming tomorrow. i know you don't want to ever come. Let's stop playing these fucking games. You want a poem? Kiss my motherfucking ass, Bitch.

David

Happy Birthday, Son.

Yeah, Mama. Bake me a cake.

Mama.

It's over.

This is it.

What do I do now?

It's a joke, Mama.

A bad joke at that.

She doesn't need me.

Doesn't want me.

What is there to want?

The excitement of what the fuck is going to happen next. Life with David Lesesne Carmichael

brought to you by Vaseline Intensive Care.

What a treat.

Spence, you motherfucker—

You can stop laughing.

I finally understand

you were just too goddamned

cowardly to blow your brains out.

You should have re-enlisted, Baby,

The Cong would have gotten your ass eventually

and then you could have paid off the debt of your life, Brother Speed,

bought your freedom.

You must have been a stupid son-of-a-bitch after all

to miss an opportunity like that.

Can't you see your family sitting around waiting

for the check just like *A Raisin in the Sun.*

All your people, wearing black

singing your praises and waiting for the money

Stop laughing, Spence

I don't know what my excuse is.

September 27, 1983

Dear David,

Happy Birthday! We know it's not a very happy time but we wanted to let you know we were thinking about you. Mr. Dumas sent away for some books for you. They ought to be there soon. I'm sorry we can't be there to lighten your load. Camille loves you very much as we know you love her. We will stand by both of you as best we can.

Be strong, Son.

Affectionately,
Ophelia and Hunter Dumas

Saturday, October 2, 1983

Camille,

Happy Birthday, Baby.

I'm sorry I don't have anything else to say.

David

Saturday, October 2, 1983

Dear Mr. and Mrs. Dumas,

Thank you very much for your kindness. The books came through this morning. *Your thinking of me means so much* but it also is very hard to take. Camille and I seem to be lost. Your gift makes me feel even more unworthy and ashamed. I long to be worthy and unashamed.

Please hug Camille for me. Both of you at once.

With much respect and gratitude,

David

October 6, 1983

Camille Royce Dumas
2913 Summit Place, N.E.
Washington, DC 20002

Dear Camille Dumas:
I regret the circumstances of this correspondence. Unfortunately, Mr. Carmichael's appeal was denied. Please tell David not to worry about the money he owes me. Please encourage him to stay in touch. If he wants to seek additional representation, there are attorneys I'd be happy to recommend to him. I have sent him a copy of the ruling. I wish you both well.
Sincerely,

Geoffrey Baker Nichols
Attorney-at-Law
Date sent October 6, 1983 GBN
GBN/kr

October 12, 1983

too late

What do you want me to do? A day doesn't go by when I don't think about you. I don't want to think about you anymore. You, that So-Lo, the baby, doing life, have wrestled me to the ground. I'm dead.

Please bury me in a shady spot.

Janeece, what do I do now?

October 15, 1983
6:30 a.m.

Dear David,

I'm going to press on, just like we were married and you were pissed off with me. Because we argue doesn't mean it's over.

I got this in the mail yesterday. Can you check and make sure everything is okay with your visitors' list? Daddy's bringing me down on November 19. One month from today.

Really. We'll be there. I'll be there.

Love,
Royce

Dear Visitor:

We want to make your visit a pleasant and safe one. In the interest of safety and cleanliness, the following regulations are provided for you.

All matters relative to personal property, to include food items, shall be governed by **IOP #141**. All hand-in items prior ordered by inmates must have prior written approval prior to acceptance and must be in accordance with **IOP #141-A**. Cash or Money Orders are subject to **IOP # 142-C**. All food items must be easily searched and of a reasonable quantity. The following items are approved for Visiting Room consumption:

1. Items from fast-food restaurants , i.e., hamburgers, chicken, pizza, Chinese food, etc.
2. Shelled nuts out of the shells.
3. Potato chips, corn chips, cookies, crackers, etc. in bags or boxes
4. Shellfish must be removed from shells prior to entry.

The following items will not be allowed

1. Liquid products
2. Canned foods
3. Ice cream.

All visitors are expected to dress in moderation. No see-through garments will be allowed while visiting. Visitors are expected to be fully clothed, i.e., all under-garments and/or panty hose. Low cut garments on female guests will not be permitted. Slits in garments more than three inches are not permitted. No strapless or tube top dresses will be allowed. Boots, high heel shoes, etc., coats, will be searched. Visitors may consult **IOP regulations #140-283** for further clarification.

Your VCF Administrative Team

October 27, 1983

Dear David,
You're the only one who would understand. I've got this job to do, Urgent Fury. Coup de main. You know, slicing through quickly. This morning I saw a woman dead in the street who looked just like Camille. I ran to her, man. I had to hold her even though I knew she was not my sister. I cried. I'm all fucked up. What do I do now?

Brother G.

Tuesday, November 22, 1983

1:52 a.m.

Royce—

What the hell is going on? November 19th came and went with no word from you. Do you think this is some kind of fucking joke? i thought i was supposed to be able to depend on you. If you don't want to fucking come, don't fucking come! There's no fucking ring on your finger. i am not the one who held out some fucking fantasy about "how we can make it." i didn't know you were such a goddamned coward. Perhaps Cedrick is correct. i was never clear on how you happened to end up at the doctor's office just as i was going to trial.

FUCK YOU!

Tuesday, November 22, 1983
2:14 a.m.

Dear Mr. and Mrs. Dumas,

You have been very kind. i apologize for taking so long to write. Royce had suggested i would be seeing Mr. Dumas and i thought i would thank him in person. i think all of this is too much for Royce. Please, as i requested before, help her to stop trying. i can't take it.

Thanks again for everything.

Respectfully and with much love,

David Lee

November 28, 1983

D.

Got your letter. Listen, I'm not your second, I'm not your duelist, or your fucking amen corner.

You're right, you can't count on me.

C.

Camille, Honey? The last thing I saw in this world before crossing over was my husband's fist. It wasn't really that he hit me that hard. I just decided, I was too tired to fight anymore. I was worn out with picking myself up off the floor and finding some reason why it was my fault. I had a piece of starch in my mouth at the time. I was chewing nice and slow and something said, Janeece, no more.

Now, I wish it hadn't spoken up, that voice. Yes, I feel light and airy and everything and I get to laugh at Big Mike when he's acting the fool, but you know, I don't taste no victory.

November 30, 1983

Dear David Lee,

I'm not much of a writer but I wanted to let you know we got your letter. You're welcome, Son. Honest to God, I wish I could do more. Mrs. Dumas and I recently learned that George was involved in the invasion of Grenada. Apparently, he is missing. We are still trying to get information about him. Camille and I were planning to come see you but then we got the news. We haven't been right since. Bear with us, son, as we bear with you.

Your friend,
Hunter Leon Dumas

December 2, 1983

If this had been a different year, George might return. But he won't. We all know he won't. Another one far away and dying. David and Cedrick seem to think I was conspiratorial. They think I made reservations for him to go. David has never asked me how I felt. Everyone assumes so much. There was the perfunctory rubbing of my abdomen. The people in the hospital acted like it didn't matter. One more little boy . . . gone . . . as if he had not left a trail of blood behind in my bedroom. I don't think I was supposed to, but I saw him lying in that little tray. His arms were spread. His face was calm, his eyes were shut. I was grateful for that. Someone had been sloppy and not gotten rid of the body or taken him right after he was expelled. I wanted to scoop him up and let him sail down some river to the sea. I'd like to set them all sailing.

Monday, December 5, 1983
4:00 p.m.

Baby—

i'm trying very hard not to lose it in here. i'm sorry for the things i said. Why didn't you tell me about George? i know, the things i can't do anything about i'd just as soon not know. What can i tell you? i love you.

David

P.S. Camille, please write.

December 9, 1983

Since I went to see him back in September, it's gotten worse. I feel nauseated all the time. The line between us won't stay still. I have felt him up in my chest. I have watched men in a different way. And now George.

Yesterday there was a man on the street I couldn't turn my back on. He was a big man. It was hot. He was wearing a dress shirt, suspenders, and dark, heavyweight trousers. He wore old spit-polished Florsheims. We went into the same store. I lingered at the checkout so that he would pass me and I could watch him. He reached for his handkerchief and the move was so full that he could have been choking someone just as easily as wiping the sweat from his neck. A few months ago, I would have given him a lot of room. Instead I followed him closely and felt something of him in me. I knew that was because of David in me. He turned and looked at me a couple of times. A month ago, I would have turned away but yesterday I met his stare and held it. That was because of George in me. Maybe if I discover the secrets the baby left in me, I could become an assassin.

December 10, 1983

I want to break him out.

December 11, 1983

I have begun preparations. A credit card for the rental car. Food. A place. An identity.

Who am I fooling? I couldn't hide now if my life depended on it. I walk around like I'm carrying David on my back. Who wouldn't spot me in a crowd unless we go to Grenada.

December 12, 1983

I haven't answered his last two letters. I still feel like I'm carrying him, but now he feels dead inside me.

I miss his kicking but I want the pieces of David in me out. I am desperate to have only me in my body.

I wonder if that's possible. I wonder if it ever was.

Cedrick would have a field day with this.

December 13, 1983

On the way to my parents', I saw a man standing on the Taylor Street bridge. I caught his eye just as he was stepping off into the traffic. I couldn't swerve. I could only put on the brakes. The low pressure in my rear tire made the car pull hard to the left. When I stopped, the bumper was against his leg. He didn't move. I had to back up and creep around him. I pulled over and waited to feel something. I didn't look around. I didn't look into the mirror.

On the way home he lay covered—all but his sneakers—a couple of yards from the spot where we had danced. The lights of the ambulance and police cars made it like Star Search. I wanted to hurt him.

December 17, 1983

I went to the porn shop and bought a dildo and a strap. I put it on at home and walked around trying to think what it might mean to be so exposed—compelled to act on something, threatened and threatening. I stood watching myself in the hall mirror and tried to think how you give birth to yourself without a womb. With a womb for that matter.

I want to know who David is. I want to know who my father is. I want to know who George is. I want to know them before they die or before they kill me. I had not expected to write that.

Camille and Ophelia sat on the porch swing in their coats. Only their toes touched the porch. They sat with half-full glasses of lemonade in their gloved right hands. Their left hands held their stomachs. Camille felt Janeece rocking with them.

You could at least go see the boy.

Who are you?

That's Miss Janeece, Momma. David Lee's mother.

Leave her alone. If she wants to see him, she will.

I don't know why I have to go see him when he's walking around in my body?

How would you feel if your son were crying for help and no one offered any?

He is. I know he is but there's nothing I can do. All I can do is wait. And pray.

Do you pray for David Lee, Camille?

No, I'm sorry I don't. Not any more.

Are you telling me you don't love him enough to pray for him?No. I'm telling you I don't know what to pray for. Not for David anyway. Right now, I'm spending lots of time praying for myself.

I guess he was right, you don't want him.

No, he's wrong. I do. It just doesn't matter what I want.

It always matters.

You don't believe that anymore than I do. If it mattered, you wouldn't have seen a grave at 39. Am I right or wrong?

You're right . . . You're dangerous.

Umm-umm. I sure am. Don't you think so, Momma?

Yes. I'd say all of us are dangerous now.

What you mean?

Ain't no rules that ain't already been broken.

Amen.

December 19, 1983

I had borrowed one of George's high school sweat shirts and an old pair of his sneakers from my parents' basement. Momma had packed his things with cedar chips but still the sweat shirt smelled of George's lime aftershave.

Last night I layered myself in as many shirts as I could until my breasts were indiscernible. I put on as many sweat pants as I could until what was below my waist was unknown. I stuffed George's Converse with newspaper and wore them. I pulled his sweat shirt around me and went out looking for the company of men. Behind the Amoco station, in the clearing near the Goodwill Store, I stood in the night with men. They let me say nothing. We watched people go by. We drank. We stood by the fire. We never got warm.

When I got home, I drew a bath. I didn't feel dirty or clean. It was too hot. I had to wait to get in. I paced the apartment looking at it as if it were not mine.

Finally, I climbed into the tub. I filled the sponge with water and let it drip over my hair and face. Blood from my cycle tinged the water.

December 20, 1983

Dear David and Camille,

I've been tearing up your letters.

I haven't been able to bring you through and I don't want to die in labor.

I'm going to leave you alone. I'm leaving you. I'm alone. I'm you. You alone. Is bad poetry relevant?

December 25, 1983

I am ready for my male relations to disembark.

Today will be my birthday.

I threw away the dildo last night. I put it and the strap in a trash can outside of a 7-11. I didn't want anyone going through my garbage and making any assumptions. I've been thinking about that little baby in that tray. Sailing down a river. I like that. Somebody's General Moses the next time around.

December 26, 1983

4:30 a.m.

Royce—

You need to motherfucking write me. Shit is *very, very* tense here. Please, baby, I need to hear from you. I need to see you. I need to have *somebody* who's got my back. I need to have someone who will write. I have written myself all the words I can.

David

January 9, 1984

I called the prison. He's in lockdown. I'm in lockdown. I thought about going down there to try and work it out but why bother. It's over. At this point, the only one I want to think about is George.

January 20, 1984

Dearest David,

I was thinking of our first meeting. You and your family hadn't been at the Perry Family Reunion picnic five minutes before you punched me in the eye. I never understood why you did that. You already had my attention. Before the day was over, you were the first boy I ever kissed. I want to have your back. I'm just not up to the duty. I' m sorry.

Love,
for what it's worth—

Camille

P.S. George was found dead on January 12th. His head was bashed in behind a bar in Point Salines. He was found in civilian clothes. I figured you'd want to know. They're sending his body home in two days.

P.P.S. Enclosed is the letter I should have written your father and your brother a long time ago. I sent it off yesterday. I send it to you for good reasons and bad ones. Don't read it, if you are afraid.

Correspondence Regulations

Mail Will Not Be Delivered Which Does Not Conform With These Rules:

No. 1. Only 2 Letters Each Week, Not To Exceed 2 Sheets Letter-Size 8 1/2 x 11" And Written On One Side Only And If Ruled Paper, Do Not Write Between Lines. Your Complete Name Must Be Signed At The Close Of Your Letter. Clippings, Stamps, Letters From Other People, Stationery Or Cash Must Not Be Enclosed In Your Letters

No 2. All Letters Must Be Addressed With The Complete Prison Name Of The Inmate. Cell Number, Where Applicable, And Prison Number Must Be Placed In Lower Left Corner Of Envelope With Your Complete Name And Address In The Upper Left Corner

No. 3. Do Not Send Any Packages Without A Package Permit. Unauthorized Packages Will Be Destroyed

No. 4. Letters Must Be Written in English Only

No. 5. Books, Magazine, Pamphlets, And Newspapers Of Reputable Character Will Be Delivered Only If Mailed Direct From The Publisher Or Pre-Approved Bookseller.

No. 6. Money Must Be Sent In The Form Of Postal Money Orders Only With The Inmate's Complete Prison Name And Prison Number.

Your VCF Administrative Team

January 19, 1984

Dear Mr. Carmichael:

You and Cedrick have tried to fill his head with every lie about me you can think of. And you have covered up your own ugly deeds. But I don't care anymore. I don't care because I finally realized in the scheme of things you are small. You are infinitesimal. You can't even save yourselves.

God help you. As much as I hate you, I know you didn't make yourselves.

C. R. Dumas

P.S. I talked to my mother and father about you last night. I have already sent off David's copy of this letter. Do what you will.

January 21, 1984

When I think of George, I always think of Grampa Hunter. Grampa Hunter was never without his measuring tape, a pencil, and small pad in his pocket. He gave George a set to carry in his pocket. Each time we'd go to see Gramps, he'd greet us with that fisted walk of his—moving like he rotated invisible handles at his hips. He would show George all of his new projects and schematics for his inventions. It seemed like overnight he went from talking about sensing devices to mistaking George for Daddy. George hated the idea that Gramps could leave him. Grampa Hunter stopped carrying his pad and measuring tape. George threw his away. Gramps stopped wearing his teeth and George stopped visiting.

The last time George and I saw him, Gramps looked like he could be held like a baby. He had a child's fear in his eyes. Gramps held the covers tightly beneath his chin. When George leaned down to kiss him good-bye, Gramps said, "This is a lot harder than I thought."

January 30, 1984

I've been staying over at Taylor Street. Lots of Daddy's old friends came to George's service. Afterwards, they played cards late into the night, casting shadows that made them look like giants smoking Phillies and drinking whiskey. They wore their cards like ashes on their foreheads. Plays swooped across the table like low-flying birds. They took solace in each other's company. Every sentence was a consoling challenge. They spoke loudly, patted their chests, laughed, and banged the table.

"Don't tell me, if he had been a white man there's just no tellin how far he could've gone."

"If he had been a white man who says he would've known where to go."

The card playing was hard on Momma.

Around 2 a.m., they fell asleep, scattered about the living room like soldiers on bivouac. All except Daddy who held on to Momma and cried with her throughout the night. I covered Daddy's friends with blankets, checked the doors, and left the light on over the stove in the kitchen.

February 4, 1984

I drove down to Richmond early this morning to see David and to tell him good-bye. I had no trouble with the guards but David would not see me.

Last night, I planned out everything I was going to say, but the closer I got to Richmond, the more the rehearsed words seemed foolish. By the time I was climbing the VCF steps, I just wanted to embrace him, touch him. My feelings hadn't changed, there just weren't enough words for who we have been to each other. I wanted to kiss him good-bye not tell him good-bye.

Momma had packed a gargantuan lunch and Daddy had loaded me down with flares, maps, flashlights, guide books, and mace. When I left their house this morning, they lingered at the car door for a long time.

"Bye, Baby."

"Drive safe."

"You have any problems, you call."

"When you be home?"

"Did you check the oil?"

"Got a full tank?"

"Here's my AAA card."

"All right, now . . ."

"We love you."

"Stop along the way in a nice motel if you get sleepy. Here's a little extra in case of an emergency."

"Bye, bye . . ." They waved slowly and Momma bit her lip.

George's death was in their eyes.

Instead of going home, I drove around Richmond for a while then I decided to drive down to the Dismal. I called Momma and Daddy to let them know my plans. I started out on highway 64. The four-lane thoroughfare was dizzying. Even the slow lanes were moving well over 70. I got off and took route 60 south. Providence. Forge. Lightfoot. Williamsburg. Jamestown. It was awkward driving. I was trying to study the scenery as I drove along unfamiliar road. And I was distracted, thinking about who I would have been 100, 200, 300 years ago and who I am today. I passed by the exit for the Busch Gardens Theme Park and laughed. The Old Country. Brewery tours, roller coasters, and 17th century Europe. I crossed the James River at Rescue. I got turned around a couple of times. It was cold but I kept the window open, hoping for the almost home smell of the Chesapeake Bay. I finally found my way to route 17 and the Dismal Swamp Canal. By the time I got there, the sun was setting. I pulled the car into one of the overlooks. There was a pier by the canal. The bare trees reflected in the winter water made it hard not to think about life on this side and the other. The wide canal was a diamond pattern of water and land. Overtures and closures. Coherence and separation.

I stood for a long time trying to imagine the people who had waded in that water, cut through the dense trees, dug the long canals, and rejoiced secretly in the Dismal's victory. Maybe it just seemed like a long time because of the seduction of the growing darkness.

I thought of men and women running; tagged but running. I could see them wearing tongue restraints, collars, and property helmets. I imagined them trying to live apart and together. I thought about husbands celebrating the release from another man's reach. Then thinking about food, shelter, and a future.

And I thought about babies stillborn under cypress trees. Babies sailing down the Albermarle Channel to Curitock Sound down to the sea, trying to get home.

I thought about what it might have meant to come to this place all alone—no mate, no mother, no father, no children.

I stood and tried to see myself in the water. You could smell the salt air.

When I left, I almost drove off the road trying to avoid a dead heron on the highway. Whose little baby child?

George, I used to be so jealous of you. Your peace. The ease of your choices. I have tried to write your parents but my jumbled feelings cloud my condolences. I envy you as I envy my son. Your escapes. You would think I would have pages to write to your father. I know his sorrow and his mournfulness. I know, not because you are son but because you are Child. Possibility. Future. Continuation. Rebellion. I know because you are Dream. Defined within our minds, not theirs. I know because you are Target, Marked and fragile. Target child dream—we run with you pressed close.

Perhaps you were not who I believed. Perhaps your ending is like mine. Talk to me, George. Tell me if you died trying to be someone you never expected. Tell me if you got caught up in what someone else had written. Tell me what steps I can take. Tell me how to let your sister be a kite. Tell me how to let our strings go. Tell me how to see her as a bird. Tell me how to make a bridge, a place, an island. Here.

February 19, 1984

Dearest Camille—my friend

First, some Neruda for you from "Letter on the Road." I had too hard a time typing the Spanish.

Farewell, but you will be
with me, you will go within
a drop of blood circulating in my veins
or outside, a kiss that burns my face
or a belt of fire at my waist
My sweet accept
the great love that came out of my life
and that in you found no territory
like the explorer lost
in the isles of bread and honey.
I found you after
the storm,
the rain washed the air
and in the water
your sweet feet gleamed like fishes.

Finally, two poems of my own for you.

Beloved, what I know of love struggles for this page
My hands are bloodied with the slaughter
and yet I dare devotion.

Can your hands crimson with birth feel the shape
of my misgivings?
They are not all I have to offer.

There are doves outside the window
Repeating my longing
My treacheries and my abuse
My loyalty and disgrace

Dream with me away from the mournful
Songs of my making
Help me transgress the bounden reading of our lives.

Can we live apart without tragedy?
We can unmake our tragedies. With tears
Without tears and yet still be vulnerable
To the pain and suffering of our stories

You who are not replaceable
May I hold your look of love?
I will cradle it gently.

Would that language were enough to speak pleasure
Sympathy, connectedness, and my sad ambivalence.

Today it is enough.

# # #

There is a place beyond my father's house that is calm
where straw-colored sunlight filters through
the trees and makes a church.
Mama dances barefoot in the
warm mix of earth and wet leaves
I have stashed my memories there
I believe they are safe.

There is a place beyond my father's house
where our son watches Mourning Cloak
butterflies while I eat red pears
and our daughter sings without quavering.

We make love in that place
and there Camille can rest
away from the phantoms that jerk her from sleep
We are people there.

There is a place beyond my father's house
where he cannot reach us
where his sickle-like arm does not slice at our roots
and I do not need to copy him
with desperate, machete gestures of my own.

There is a place beyond my father's house
where even he can be at peace
watching our mothers dance
and smelling the sea.

# # #

"Adored one, I am off to my fighting"

Good luck with your own. I will be fine.

Your friend—

David Lesesne Carmichael

Me here. All chilren here. Maa. Okànràn òdí ní èmi kò gbodò ní àyà jíjá. No Maa. Heart no afraid.

212. Elviretta Scott, a freed black

213. Conchetta Scott, a freed black

214. Vondas Scott, a freed black

215. Victor Hugo Scott, a freed black

216. Althea Scott, a freed black

217. Michellin Jackson, a freed black

218. Emerald Blue, a freed black

219. Christmas Worth, a freed black

220. Gazette Hart, a free man of color

221. Eppie, a slave

222. Joe Nita, a slave

223. Easter, a slave

224. Canada, a free woman

225. Ned, a slave

226. Lovey Griffin, a free woman

227. Henry, a slave

228. Bob, a slave

229. Stobo James, a freed black

230. Egypt Flanders, a free woman

231. Benjamin Coleman, a free man of color

232. Connecticut Walker, a freed black

233. *Obed, a slave*

234. *Custy, a slave*

235. *The Clarkson Family - 63 members*

236. *The Pleasant Family of Augusta, Georgia - 57 members*

237. *Prince Hugh, a freed black*

238. *Holloway Price, a freed black*

239. *Nat, a slave*

240. *Rose Foster, a freed black*

241. *Maria Holmes and children, freed blacks*

242. *Vernina Johns, a freed black*

243. *Saphronia, a slave*

244. *Luther Mack, a freed black*

245. *Frances World, a freed black*

About the Author

Monifa A. Love was born in 1955 in Washington, D.C., and graduated with honors from Princeton. Her collection of poetry, *Provisions,* was published by Lotus Press in 1989. She is the recent recipient of a Ph.D. in English from The Florida State University.